Kiss my firm but pliant lips

# Kiss my
# firm but pliant lips
## Dan Greenburg

Grossman Publishers

New York

*for Laurie*

Kiss my firm but pliant lips

# 1

I, Oliver Bloom, a nice young man with an unnecessarily vulnerable face, lay on my plaid beach blanket, practicing noninvolvement.

I stared into the very bright reflection of the sun on the ocean. I savored the calm of the sparsely settled beach.

By and by, a nice slender lady who was not quite pretty came walking down the sand by the water with a nice German shepherd who was not quite a pure German shepherd but who carried himself nicely.

The not quite pure German shepherd spotted my narrow white body and frolicked over. Straddling my torso, he vigorously licked my face and wagged my knees with his tail.

"Your average dog is sorely in need of an effective mouthwash," I called to the lady.

The not quite pretty lady approached uncertainly.

"I'm sorry," she said. "Albert is very interested in new things."

A heavy paw was placed experimentally on my chest.

"I am not what you might call a new thing," I said, "being essentially twenty-eight years of age."

"Twenty-eight is nice," said the lady wistfully. "Albert is twenty-four, and I thirty-one. Months and then years, I mean."

"I got the large animal's name," I said, "but not that of his friend."

"Just 'Albert's Friend' is good enough," said the lady. "You don't have to tell every jerk who lies on the beach your name."

"Fine," I said, placing Albert's left paws firmly alongside his right ones and rolling over on my stomach.

"I didn't say that to be rude, but merely stated a personal viewpoint."

"Good," I said.

"I truly am sincerely sorry. I mean that."

"Fine."

"May I sit here for a few moments and restore your jolly mood, not on the nice plaid blanket but only on the sand?"

"Sure," I said. 'It's not *my* sand."

"Now then," said the lady. "I shall begin by telling you how I met my husband who is now dead of an affliction of the liver. Baby was his name. Not his first, you understand, but his last. My husband's full name was Harry Baby. That makes me Mrs. Baby. Don't you find that amusing?"

"Very amusing."

"Good, you're getting happier already. I can tell. Anyway, the way I met Harry Baby was driving down Wilshire Boulevard. Harry was in the left lane. I didn't *know* it was Harry then, I mean, but there he was, with his left thing blinking. His *turning* dealie—you know."

"I know," I said.

"The second I saw him I grew weak. He had this very tiny head. Everybody called him Baby Harry, of course. And those eyes! Well, what was I to do? Here I had just met the only man I would ever love, and he was about to make a left turn right out of my life. So what did I do? What *could* I do?"

She poked me in the small of the back. "Come on, what did I do?"

"Search me, lady," I said.

"Well, I cut my wheels hard to the left, stepped on the whaddayacallit—the gas dealie—and smashed in his right door. Quick thinking?"

5

"Quick thinking," I said and rolled over to look at the lady. "What was Harry Baby's reaction, exactly?"

"Well, you know Harry."

"No," I said, "I don't."

"I mean he said a lot of vile things. I suppose he felt it was expected of him. Then he asked me how it happened, and I told him I couldn't think of any other way to meet him. That's when he fell in love with me. So then we got married and then he developed this affliction in the liver and died. Do you mind very much if I sit on your blanket? This sand is grainy."

"Help yourself," I said.

She did.

Albert moved tentatively back to my chest as the lady sat down, but I gently pushed him flat on the blanket. He authorized my action with a perfunctory lick of my wrist.

"There now," said the lady, placing the large wicker basket which served as her purse beside her. "Now you tell me about you."

"Nothing to tell," I said. "I'm twenty-eight, unemployed, and a little sunburned on the nose and forehead."

"Married?"

"Nope."

"Planning to be married?"

"Nope."

"Like to be married?"

"Not particularly."

6

"I bet you're a marvelous lover."

"Passable."

"You're being modest."

"Yes."

"Would you like to make love to me? I don't mean *will* you—*would* you is really what I had in mind. A theoretical question."

"I don't know. I suppose. I don't know."

"Why don't you know? Don't you think I'm attractive?"

"I guess. What do you want me to say?"

"I don't *want* you to say *any*thing. I merely asked whether you thought I was an attractive person or not."

"Sure. You're attractive enough."

"But you don't find me . . . appealing."

"Appealing?"

"I mean to *you*. Personally."

"Oh sure. You're appealing enough."

"Enough for what?"

"Enough for . . . I don't know. You're very attractive and you're very appealing, O.K.?"

"Would you say my eyes are haunting?"

"Haunting?"

"Yes, Harry always said my eyes were haunting."

"Well, I suppose you could say they were haunting, yes. Quite haunting, as a matter of fact."

"You're not just saying that because you wish to be cordial?"

"No, not at all."

7

"Now, what about my hair?"

"Your hair?"

"Yes. Is it radiant? Harry always said I had radiant hair."

"Madam, I would say your hair is approximately blinding."

"You're a hell of an attractive man, you know that?"

"Thank you. Thank you very much."

"Too bad you don't like me."

"What makes you say I don't like you?"

"I can tell. You're just being kind and not wanting to hurt my feelings."

"That's ridiculous. I like you very much. In fact, I like you so much it pains me to even think about it."

"That is very beautiful. I wish I could believe you."

"You have my solemn word of honor."

"Will you do me a favor?"

"Anything."

"First, come here. Move Albert."

"Done and done," I said. I slid Albert to the extreme right edge of the blanket and squeezed in between him and his friend.

"Second, place your left arm lovingly about my cream-white shoulders."

"Like so?" I engulfed her cream-white shoulders.

"Third, give me a tender kiss on my firm but pliant lips."

I kissed her firm but pliant lips.

All at once the lady turned and gave me a violent shove. I landed on Albert, who appeared genuinely

8

amazed. He growled. I pulled myself off Albert and stood up.

"What the hell was *that* for?" I demanded.

"Help!" shrieked the lady.

"Shhh!" I said.

"Police!" said the lady.

"Shut up, for God's sake," I hissed.

"Criminal assault!" said the lady.

"Oh, dear sweet God in heaven," I said.

"Help! Help! Police!"

A few curious people approached from up the beach.

"Help! Police! Help!" called the lady. "Somebody get the police!"

Albert snarled fiercely.

A faint puttering sound drifted over the sand. Presently, a uniformed officer appeared on a three-wheeled motorcycle.

"Help!" said the lady. "Help!"

"What the hell's going on here?" said the policeman, striding up to the blanket.

"This man tried to attack me!"

"That true, buddy?"

"Hell no!" I said.

"How's that again?"

"Heck no, sir," I said.

"He sat down on my blanket and put his arms around me and tried to kiss me—ask anybody!"

"She is completely out of her pumpkin," I said. "And that is *my* blanket, not hers."

"That true, lady?" said the policeman.

9

"He put his arms around me and tried to kiss me with his mouth. Naturally I pushed him away. Have you ever seen anything like that before, officer?"

"Every day," said the officer. "Every day. You want to press charges or what?"

"Wait a minute!" I said.

"Shut up!" said the officer. "You want to press charges, lady?"

"Heavens, no. Just get him out of here, that's all."

"You heard her, buddy—vamoose!"

"Not until I get my blanket. That's my blanket. I'm not leaving without my blanket." I spread my legs to a wider stance and folded my arms across my chest.

"He says it's his blanket," said the policeman.

"He's crazy. Are you going to believe every crazy jerk on a beach who says it's his blanket?"

"*She's* the one who's crazy," I said. "I was just lying here, watching the water, when she comes up with this crazy Albert and tells me about her crazy husband, Harry Baby, and asks if she can sit down, and asks me to put my arms around her cream-white shoulders, and asks me to kiss her firm but pliant . . . It's *true!* I swear to God!"

"Sure," said the policeman, "sure."

"He is utterly insane," said the lady.

"Grrulff!" said Albert.

"Now then," said the policeman, "I don't care if the lady wants to press charges or not, I am personally taking you back to the station on my nice three-wheeled motorcycle and locking you up very tight unless you are off this beach in three seconds flat. One!"

"You're all out of your gourds," I said, "you, her, and Albert also."

"Two!"

"May I at least have my *Sea and Ski?*"

"Three!"

"I'm going, I'm going!" I said and marched haughtily away from the blanket and into the water and all the way up to my collarbone before removing my B. F. Goodrich sneakers.

It is hardly possible to remain submerged in sea water up to the level of your eyeballs for two consecutive hours without experiencing a certain dampening of the spirits.

Albert and the widow Baby kept lying and lying on my plaid beach blanket with such obvious relish that I began to suspect they had discovered some erotic content in the tartan of Ancient Buchanan.

I remained crouching seven-eighths below the surface of the Pacific Ocean, like a sneaky offshore iceberg, though I suppose that "crouch" is not really an apt description of what it is icebergs do seven-eighths below the surface of the ocean. If someone had come along and asked me what I was doing, I probably would have had to consider a long while before replying.

My plan was a bit vague at the time. It involved the recapture of my blanket. It involved some sort of reparation for the humiliating scene with the policeman. It was bound up with alternate feelings of rage, despair, awe, and even admiration for the lady who had so skillfully directed the brief production on shore. My plan also presupposed the ability to observe the lady undetected until she left the beach and I could confront her in an environment slightly less accessible to officers of the law and curious passersby.

About a third of the way into my moist vigil, I became aware of the fact that I still held, a foot or two below the water line, the sneakers I had removed upon entering the ocean. After a moment of serious debate, I put them back on and tied the laces, scrupulously avoiding drowning in the process.

As the sun began to set, I grew somewhat more than chilly. The fact that I was clad in shoes, socks, shorts and a Joe Weeder Tight-Fit T-Shirt scarcely lessened the chill.

I was therefore rather pleased to note the lady and her dog begin the process of standing up, shaking out, and going home. When my plaid beach blanket had been carefully folded and tucked under her arm, the lady turned, walked briskly to the edge of the water, cupped her hands to her mouth, and called like thousands of California mothers to their waterlogged babies at the end of a fun-filled day at the beach: "Come on in, dear, it's time to go home!"

There was absolutely no doubt about it. I was the only kid in the water.

Sheepishly, I uncrouched and made my way in to shore.

"A person who does not know when to come out," said the lady, noting the essentially turquoise tint of my skin, "should never be allowed in."

I began an observation that a person who commandeered another person's personal effects was hardly in any appropriate ethical or moral position to judge that person's qualifications to do *any*thing, but my teeth were chattering so badly that only alternate syllables escaped my lips.

"Dry up first; we'll talk later," said the lady and, with an unequivocal nudge from Albert, I was escorted to the parking area and the relative aridity of their waiting Morris Minor.

# 2

When one is involved in so personal and emotional an act as dying, there is scarcely anything so annoying as someone else standing around being practical. That was my thought as I leaned against the doorjamb of Mrs. Baby's neo-modern house.

"Come on in the john," said the lady. "You're still dripping pretty good, and the carpet is not color-fast."

She steered me into the lavatory and deposited me on the commode.

15

"Now then, here is my late husband's terry-cloth bathrobe. You want to undress yourself, or don't you think you can handle it altogether?"

I pondered the question gravely for fully two minutes, then, unable to think of any snappy rejoinder, I groaned and slid onto the tiled floor.

"I haven't got enough troubles, I have to wet-nurse every jerk on the beach who thinks he drowned," said the lady, efficiently divesting me of sneakers, socks, shirt and shorts. When she began to tug at my skivvies, a deep-seated sense of modesty lent me the strength to protest.

"Hey," I croaked.

"Hey yourself," said the lady. "Dry, you can recuperate on Albert's sofa. Wet, you can lie here all night for all I care."

I closed my eyes in submission.

"Frankly," she said, easing me out of my Fruit-of-the-Looms, "I got less interest in your personal fixtures than I got in my own bathtub faucet."

She rolled my clothes into a soggy ball and stood up.

"Soon as I dump these in the dryer and make up the sofa, I'll come back and get you. Don't go away."

And then she was off on her mission of mercy, leaving me uncovered on the tiles. To pass the time, I drifted off into delirium.

A minute or a month later, it was hard to tell which, I heard a pronounced snuffling above my head. I opened my eyes and through a fevered fog beheld Albert's large furry face peering quite interestedly into my own. Sensing the basic vulnerability of my person at that moment, I decided not to make any rude references to the condition of his breath. If he needed to see his dentist, let one of his best friends tell him. I was hardly more than a nodding acquaintance.

Albert's snuffling inspection began with my nose, proceeded along my right cheek to my ear, down my neck to my clavicle and thence to my armpit, which he seemed to find more than a little amusing. The expedition proceeded southerly to my belly button. I groaned, Albert growled, and I experienced the first vague stirrings of hysteria.

Just then the lady returned.

"Albert, for God's sake," she said and bums-rushed him out the bathroom door.

"O.K.," she said to me, "upsadaisy."

She grabbed me under the armpits and with astonishing ability lifted me off the floor, dragged me into a dimly lit room near the back of the house and tucked me between the sheets of a freshly made-up bed.

She placed the inside of her wrist against my forehead, then pulled it away as if scalded. "You're on *fire*, for God's sake," she said.

I closed my eyes, opened them and she was gone.

I closed them again, opened them and she was back.

"Open up," she said, forcing something between my teeth.

"Wha' izzit?" I asked.

**17**

"Anacin," she said. "C'mon, open up. Fast fast incredibly fast relief. Open up, for God's sake, you wanna die?"

I opened up.

"Swallow."

I swallowed. It might have been easier with water.

"That's a good boy. What's your name, lover?"

"Ollr," I said.

"Ollr?" she said.

"Ollvr," I said.

"Oliver?" she said.

"Mmmm," I said. "Whassyours?"

"What?"

"Whass *your* name?"

"Bernice," she said, leaning in close and scalding her lips on my forehead. "Bernice. But you can call me Mrs. Baby."

Bernice and Albert tended me diligently during the next three or four days. Unfortunately, I was not able to be present for the greater part of the time, and when I was it was under extenuating circumstances—I was out of my skull on Anacin and fever. I would often awake to see brown eyes soulfully watching me (whether Albert's or Bernice's I wasn't able to figure), and once I revived to the realization that somebody was rubbing my chest with mayonnaise (which must have been Bernice—Albert didn't like me that well yet).

So I simmered under a low flame for about forty-eight hours, and then I awoke and the fever was gone. So were my bones, as I discovered when I tried to sit up. I lay back on the pillow and tried to remember where I might have left them.

By and by, Bernice tippytoed into the room in a terry-cloth robe.

"Well!" she said, noting my wakeful state. "And how are we today?"

"You, we don't know. I, not overly bad."

"Sit up. Stick out your tongue."

I didn't sit up, but I did stick out my tongue. Also I waggled my fingers at her, thumbs in ears.

"All of a sudden we're peppy as a pup. Albert, look how peppy he is."

Albert poked his nose in and looked, but if he noted any similarity between me and peppy pups, he was keeping his own counsel.

"Sit up," said Bernice, "can't you?"

"First give me back my bones."

"Poor baby. Are you really that weak?"

"I am really that weak."

Bernice turned on a curious new sort of smile, walked over to the sofa and sat down.

"You really can't move. Do you mind if I sit next to you?"

"It's your sofa, lady."

She shifted slightly and then she was sitting *so* next to me I couldn't breathe. She ran the back of her hand contemplatively over my cheek and then pulled it away and examined it for contusions.

"You've got a pretty good stubble for five days, pal,"

she observed. "Also you come on a little heavy in the sweat department."

"You invited your*self* to sit down, as I recall."

"Don't get me wrong," she replied, as I began to get her wrong, "personally, I'm very fond of stubble. Also sweat."

"In that case, you've got yourself a winner."

"I know. Harry used to be that way at the beginning, all stubbly and sweaty. It was marvelous. We'd make love all the time—here, in the bedroom, on the bathroom floor, in the car, on top of the freezer, anywhere. Albert was very intrigued."

"I'll bet he was."

"But then, something began to go wrong. Harry got a job. Every morning he'd hop out of bed, shave, shower and put on talcum. I couldn't stand to touch him during the week at all. It would take the whole weekend to get him back into shape, and then it would be Monday again and out would come the old razor and soap and talcum, and it was all over for another week."

"Poor child. How you must have suffered."

"Easy it wasn't. Have you ever tried to make love to talcum? Johnson's Baby Powder, he had to have. At first I figured it was some kind of a gag to go with his name —Harry Baby? Then I discovered he actually *liked* the stuff. I don't know. It's a terrible thing to say, but I was almost grateful when he contracted whooping cough and went to his eternal reward."

"Whooping cough? I thought you said he died of an affliction of the liver."

"Well, what's the difference. He was so smooth-shaven and soapy smelling and powdered up when he died, all the undertaker had to do was rouge his cheeks and pump in the formaldehyde. Harry wasn't sick a day in his life until he started cleaning up. I think all that rubbing and polishing was what finally wore him down."

"You seriously believe there's a connection between health and grubbiness?"

"Of course. Look at cave men. Look at your goddam Cro-Magnon man. Did *he* know from Johnson's Baby Powder? Was he healthy?"

"Yeah. Up until the age of about twenty-six. Then he grew senile or was eaten by a tiger. Life expectancy wasn't too hot in those days."

"Where'd you hear that? I thought they lived about a hundred and fifty years. I thought they were real old guys."

"I'm afraid not. They never lived more than about twenty-five or thirty years. Trust me."

"Yeah? What about the Bible guys—Abraham and Moses and Adam—all those guys. *They* lived about a hundred and fifty years."

"Well, they had a different system of keeping time. According to the standards we go by, however, their average life expectancy wasn't more than about forty years."

"Go on."

"Honest."

"How do you know?"

21

"I read it somewhere."

"Yeah? Well, *I* read somewhere that they lived to a hundred and fifty without any trouble at all. One guy —Methuselah, I think—made it all the way up to nine hundred."

"Well anyway, your theory doesn't seem to work for me. I'm pretty big, stubblewise *and* odorwise, and I'm weak as a newborn kitten."

The curious smile returned.

"Listen," she said, "you mind if I slip out of my robe? I'm all dressed underneath."

She didn't wait for permission. And dressed meant bra and flowered panties.

"Very nice with the pants," I said. "Are they jonquils or philodendrons?"

"Ohrbach's," she said, drew back the covers and hopped in beside me.

"Maybe you didn't hear before. I told you I'm too weak to move."

"Who asked you to move? All I want is a little huggy-bear, for God's sake. You relax. I'll hug."

I relaxed. She hugged. It wasn't too fulfilling, but it *was* nice in a quiet kind of way.

Suddenly, I thought I heard a noise.

"Hey," I whispered, "I thought I heard a noise."

No reply.

"Hey," I said a little louder, "did you hear a noise?"

"I didn't hear a thing," she said directly into my eardrum, "I'm mainly hugging."

As it was I who was looking in the direction of the doorway, it was I who saw him first.

A big guy. Dark. Nicely groomed.

"Bernice," I said *sotto voce*, "who's that?"

Bernice stopped hugging and looked up.

"I don't see a thing," she said.

The guy never moved.

"In the doorway," I said.

"I don't see a thing," she said.

I was almost ready to write the guy off as post-fever hallucination when he opened his mouth and decided to speak. It wasn't directed to either one of us. It was a general announcement.

"Hi," he said. "Harry's home."

# 3

Now, I would like to get something straight right here. I am a very blasé guy. I worked very hard to become a very blasé guy, and it took a lot of patience, but it did pay off. I am probably as blasé as the first fifty blasé guys you will chance to come across on any major street in any major city west of the Alleghenies. By that I mean very few things truly surprise me, or *appear* to surprise me, which may be more to the point. They may *irritate* me. They may *annoy* me. They may drive me *crazy*. But very few things really *surprise* me.

I admit that when I looked up from Bernice's basic huggy-bear and saw this guy standing in the doorway I was not *expecting* him. I admit that. Nobody had said anything about company coming, so I was not *expecting* him. But I can truthfully say that when I saw him *I was not surprised*. I have been around and about just long enough to have had people walk in on me at all conceivable inopportune moments, and I believe I can say with some authority that having people walk in on you when you are entertaining a young lady in bed—even passively, as I was doing here—is not a surprising occurrence. As a matter of fact, I would go so far as to say that when you are entertaining a young lady in bed and someone does *not* walk in on you—*that* is a lot more like a surprising occurrence.

However, when the guy in the doorway said, "Harry's home," I have to admit it. I was surprised all to hell.

Blasé guys are not generally called upon to deal with situations of this nature. By that I mean it is very hard to be the right *degree* of blasé unless you know exactly what it is you are being blasé *about*.

When the fellow in the doorway said "Harry's home," I truly did not know whether he was (1) a passing stranger who was just correctly identifying the house as "Harry's home"; or (2) Harry himself, the lawful husband of the young lady, miraculously cured of a fatal affliction of the liver and/or whooping cough;

or (3) the cuckold ghost of Harry Baby, returned to seek his vengeance.

I decided in my sincere befuddlement to say nothing.

Bernice, for reasons best known to her, also decided to say nothing, though it is most likely she had heard and seen approximately what or whom I had, huggy-bear notwithstanding. Even if the fellow *were* a ghost, there is no reason to suppose that he might have been more visible to me than to his lawfully wedded wife.

And so, since neither I nor Bernice seemed eager to advance the conversation, the fellow took it upon himself to do so.

Looking primarily at Bernice, he said as follows:

"Honey, I'm home. It's me, Harry."

To which the lady replied:

"I don't *see* nothin', I don't *hear* nothin'. Did somebody come into my house?"

After a due period of time had elapsed, sensing that the person who had walked in on us was probably (2) Harry himself, rehabilitated, I spoke in the following manner:

"Bernice, this is your late and great husband, Harry Baby. He has somehow been healed from the ravages of an affliction of the liver and/or whooping cough and is now back in our midst. Harry, this is your wife Bernice Baby, whom I have had the pleasure of knowing briefly, though not in the Biblical sense, and who has nursed me back to health with Anacin and pure or at least ninety-nine and forty-four one-hundredths percent pure loving-

27

kindness. I am Oliver Bloom, very heavy in the sweat and stubble departments and very light in strength and blasété. As soon as I am hardy enough to walk, I shall collect my clothes, my plaid beach blanket and my wits, and I shall be on my accustomed and rather ordinary way."

"Glad to meet ya, Ollie," said Harry Baby, "and stay as long as you like. I and Bernice are very hospitable with strangers."

# 4

The day after Harry Baby came back from the dead, I was able to sit up and take nourishment. The day after that, I was able to stand up and take stock. I sensed that the moment for my departure had come.

As I was collecting my personal effects and stuffing them into my pockets, Bernice and Albert ambled into the room and sat down on the sofa.

"Bernice," I said, "I don't suppose I have to tell you that you saved my life."

"I don't suppose you do," she said.

"Well, I'm very grateful. I wish there were some way for me to return the favor. But I can't in all conscience ask you to contract pneumonia just so I can repay a kindness. In any case," I said, giving Bernice a friendly squeeze on the shoulder, and giving Albert a calculated pat on the forehead, "now I must truly be off. Perhaps we'll see each other again. One never knows."

"One never knows," said Bernice.

"Snuff," said Albert.

Waving a handkerchief, I left.

The old neighborhood hadn't changed drastically since I'd left it, some seven or nine days before. Cars without tops still lined both sides of the street, looking like a low-flying sabre jet had swooped down and lopped off their heads above the eyebrows. Hefty folks in sleeveless shirts and legless pants still strolled along, advertising great expanses of orangey skin. And all but the blind wore dark glasses.

I skipped up the steps to my tiny courtyard bungalow and slipped my key into the doorknob lock, but it didn't turn. I jiggled the key, I joggled the knob. Nothing happened. I kicked the door. It opened. A little kid stood in the opening, looking up at me with his mouth ajar. Whoever each of us had expected to see, it wasn't the other. In my own case, since I live alone, I hadn't expected to see anyone at all.

"Hello, kid," I said. "Who you?"

The kid just stared.

"May I come in?" I said.

No reply.

"Whatsamatta, kid—cat got ya tongue?" I laughed a jolly laugh.

This kid's mouth was still cocked, but nothing came out except breathing noises.

I tried a more jovial approach:

"Say, I hope you don't mind my barging in on you like this, but I just happened to be in the neighborhood and I thought I'd drop by and see what's up. How's Mildred and the girls?"

The kid was used to dealing with madmen. He remained inscrutable.

I eased my way into the room.

"Look, doctor, I know I'm late for my session. Shall I just lie down and begin where I left off yesterday?"

Nothing.

Just then a lady's voice bounced irritatedly into the room, followed by the lady herself.

"Robbie, I *told* you not to keep opening the *door,* pussycat. Mommy isn't dressed and if—*oh!*" she said, catching sight of me and trying to hide behind her arms. I don't know what she thought was showing. A lady reveals less of herself in a slip than in any outfit currently sanctioned for public daytime use in Southern California.

"Excuse me," I said, trying to make my voice as unrapelike as possible.

"Perfectly all right," said the lady, recovering her aplomb. "You came just in time. Come on," she added, leading the way into the kitchen.

"There," she said, indicating the ironing board. "See if *you* can do it."

"Do what?" I said.

She gave me a quick, suspicious glance.

"*Fix* it," she said. "What do you think I called you for?"

"I think there's been a grave misunderstanding."

Her eyes narrowed dangerously.

"You aren't going to fix it?"

"What we have here is a classic example of noncommunication—"

"What we have here is an ironing board that doesn't work."

"I don't think you fully appreciate the problem here."

"The problem is that it keeps jumping back into the wall when you want to iron on it, and it keeps flopping back down when you want to put it away."

"I know," I said, "I'm familiar with the ironing board in question. You see—"

"Well, I'm delighted to hear that. Now then, did you come here to fix it, or did you come here for some *other* purpose?"

What that other purpose might have been, I did not choose to speculate. Because if the lady had any intention of summoning the authorities, her present attire and my previous record would place me in a decidedly compromising position.

"Look," I said, adopting a clinical approach, "the key to our lack of communication in this context arises directly from an initially incorrect mutual identification of the two parties involved in the communication, or, rather, the *attempt* at communication, since any successful intercourse between two . . ."

I realized my verbal error even before the lady began backing slowly toward the sink.

"Perhaps that was a poor choice of terms," I said hastily, "though the word 'intercourse' is certainly valid in this context, meaning, as it does, an exchange of ideas or goods between two parties. It of course has, in addition, unfortunate sexual ramifications as well—unfortunate, that is, in this particular situation. My choice of the word, however, was merely a Freudian slip, of added interest here since its use carries with it the prospect of adverse repercussions and, hence, implies perhaps some sort of . . ." (the lady had reached behind her on the sink and located a heavy wrench) ". . . of a death wish on the part of . . . uh . . . of him who uttered it, which, in this case . . . uh . . . would, of course be . . . uh . . . me." I stopped babbling and assumed a breezy tone.

"Look," I said, "why don't I come back some other time when you're busier?" I began backing rapidly toward the door.

"Take one more step and I'll squish your head like a grape," said the lady evenly, and in the same tone addressed her silent son: "Robbie, pussycat, run next door and ask the landlady to call the police."

33

The cat may very well have had the little fellow's tongue, but it obviously did not have his legs. He was gone like a shot.

"Now wait," I said, "I know how this must look. But I assure you, it's not what you think. It is true I didn't come here to fix your ironing board—because it is *not* your ironing board. It's *my* ironing board. You see, the fact of the matter is that I *live* here. This is my *home.*"

The expression on the lady's face changed only slightly. She now saw that I was no simple masher. I was clearly a dangerous psychopath.

"Look," I said, "why don't you put that thing down. I'm not going to attack you. Believe me, I haven't the slightest interest in your body."

This was apparently another unfortunate choice of words. The lady's expression now contained an added ingredient: injured ego. No woman wants to be told a man finds her uninteresting—even a dangerous psychopath like myself.

"Perhaps I should rephrase that," I said. "It's not that I find you repulsive or ugly or anything like that—I don't. Quite the contrary—I find you to be a very lovely young woman, and I am sure that, had we met under other circumstances, in less troubled times, we might have had a truly stimulating and mutually satisfying relationship. However, as things stand now, it would seem that the wisest course for us to take is to part immediately—sever the relationship quickly and cleanly, while we are still able to walk away from it with our self-respect intact, and with perhaps even a few fond memo-

34

ries to carry forward into our twilight years." This last thought was gratuitous, but once I get started I find it hard to stop.

Just then the kid returned with reinforcements—several neighbors, and an assortment of blunt instruments which included my landlady.

"Why, Mr. Bloom," said she, not unkindly, "what are *you* doing back?"

"You *know* this person?" said the lady with the monkey wrench.

"Of course. This is Mr. Bloom."

"And *whom* is Mr. *Bloom?*"

"Mr. Bloom—the former tenant."

"The *present* tenant," I said.

"The *former*," said the landlady. "Oh, now, don't worry, Mr. Bloom, your sister took care of everything—the moving, the back rent—everything. I told her it was kind of short notice and all, but it just so happened *this* lady had stopped by that very morning to inquire about vacancies in furnished apartments, so, naturally, I couldn't very well hold a grudge, what with your sister paying the back rent and the redecorating and all, and so I guess everybody comes out hunky-dory, don't they?"

"*Sister?*" I said, "I don't *have* any sister."

The landlady smiled tolerantly. "Oh, go on with you now, Mr. Bloom."

"I do *not* have a sister," I said. "Cross my heart."

"Of course you do," said the landlady. "Why, I noticed the resemblance soon as she walked in the door.

The spitting image. Two peas in a pod, I swear it. That lovely Mrs. Baby."

"Mrs. *Baby,* did you say?"

"Yep, said you'd met with a bit of an accident. I do hope you're feeling better, now you're up and about." She raised her chin and sighted along her nose at me through her bifocals. "Land sakes, you sure lost weight," she said. "What did they *do* to you while you was sick?"

"That is precisely what I aim to find out," I said, parting the neighbors like Moses and passing through them to the opposite shore.

By the time I reached the house it was half-past lunch.

"Come in, come in," said Bernice from behind an apple. "You're late."

I took a deep breath. This wasn't going to be easy.

"Bernice, what do you take me for—an imbecile?"

She furrowed her brow and appeared to give the matter a good deal of thought before replying.

"Not exactly an *imbecile,*" she said seriously. "More, I'd say, like . . . simpleton?"

"Oh, for Pete's sake!" I said. "Now listen to me—"

"Addlepate? How's about addlepate?" She giggled and bit the apple.

"Very funny. Look, Bernice, I don't pretend to know what sort of kick you're getting out of all this, but the fact is that I simply won't—"

"Nincompoop. There now, that's more like it—

nincompoop. It kind of flows, you know? Nin. Come. Poop." She exploded with laughter and ended up coughing applesauce. I pounded her back.

"Thanks," she wheezed.

"You're welcome," I said. "NOW LISTEN TO ME—"

"Yes? Why, Oliver, your face is all flushed. Do you have a fever, dear? Come here, let Mommy feel."

I groaned and covered my face with my hands.

"Oh, there there. Poor *baby*." She put her arms around me and hugged. Gently. She really was a marvelous hugger.

"Bernice," I said weakly, "what do you want from me?"

"There, there. Shhh. It's all right now, baby. Mommy's here."

"Bernice, please. Just tell me what it is you want. Whatever it is, you'll probably get it anyway. Just tell me, so I'll know. It will save us both a lot of trouble. What is it, Bernice? What do you want?"

When she spoke again, her voice was no longer mocking. It was soft, very soft. And womanly. And sincere.

"I don't know, Oliver. I swear to God I don't know." She kissed my forehead. "I've got all of your earthly goods. They're in the garage. I moved them yesterday. I know you don't have any money, and I thought I could force you to stay here, but I guess even free room and board and a lien on your property for your back rent isn't going to be enough to keep you here if you really don't want to stay." She stroked my neck. "Please stay, Oliver. I like you so much. I'd like to love you, but I

37

don't guess I really know how. Maybe you can show me."

"What about Harry?"

"Harry doesn't exist. He's a figment of his own imagination. Please stay, Oliver. I'd like very much to sleep with you. Please, Oliver. Stay. I'm begging. And I've never done that out loud before."

The warm wet things on her face were tears. Real tears. I touched her eyes with my lips. And then I touched her lips. It wasn't so damned bad.

"O.K.," I said. "O.K."

I think it is important for us to examine here my feelings about moving in with Bernice. Or, rather, Bernice and Harry. Or, rather, Bernice and Harry and Albert.

First, there was this kind of curious thing I was beginning to feel for old Bernice, which was compounded of about equal parts of awe, lust, admiration, and maybe also Oedipal attraction. Not that Bernice particularly reminded me of my mother, because she didn't— my mother is not a nut. True, Bernice had about three years on me in age, and, true, Bernice did come on kind of heavy with the mother routine at times. But if she was a mother figure to me, she was also a daughter figure, and maybe even a mascot figure as well.

Then there was the problem of Harry. Whether Bernice acknowledged his existence or not, he was still her legal husband, which brought up not only a sticky moral question but also a very valid health question:

Just how healthy is it to sleep with a woman whose husband lives in the same house and outweighs you by a good eighty pounds?

The factor which tipped the balance, though, was the monetary one. You can stay on for a pretty long while in an apartment where you owe a few months' back rent and, if you have any personal magnetism at all, nobody is going to throw you out into the street. But just try finding a new place using personal magnetism as a down payment.

So, for better or for worse, for richer or for poorer, for wiser or for stupider, I moved in. Moving in, in this particular case, amounted to little more than sitting down. Whatever personal effects I owned were either in my pockets or in Bernice's garage.

Immediatly after lunch, Bernice began to make me feel right at home. She took me into the bathroom (emergency receiving room of a week or so before), opened the supply cabinet and issued me a face towel, a bath towel, a toothbrush and a bar of soap.

"You can have thirds on the morning shower schedule," she informed me. It was obvious who had firsts, but I wasn't quite sure whether it was Harry or Albert who outranked me in the number two position.

"Next order of business," she said briskly. "Breakfast is at nine, lunch is at one, and supper is when I get around to it. Everybody helps with something—what do you want, washing the dishes or drying them plus setting the table?"

"I want whatever Albert's got," I said.

"Albert helps, but not with the dishes," she said. "Don't be a smart alec."

"Bernice?"

"Yes?"

"You're, uh, really serious about all this—the top sergeant routine with the supplies, the shower schedule, the meal schedule, the K.P. duties . . . ?"

"Look, I'm running a household, right? Nobody paying bills here but me, right? What am I supposed to do, work my schedule around everybody's whims as well?"

"No, I suppose not. But still, well, I don't know. Isn't this kind of a cold-blooded attitude for a, well, at least a *potential* lover?"

She glanced at the floor for no more than a second, but when she looked back up at me it was like she had stepped behind a screen and changed her eyes: she was a woman again.

"I'm sorry, baby," she said. "Am I really that vile?"

"More or less. Hey, Sarge?"

Arms around my neck. Head tucked under my chin.

"Yes, love?"

"Where do I bunk?"

Lips on my chin. Fingers in my hair.

"With me. Where else?"

"Am I thirds on that schedule too?"

She yanked herself violently out of my arms.

"Let's get something very straight, Mr. Bloom."

"Bernice, I'm sor—"

"Let's just get something very straight right now.

Fact one: you are very far from being God's gift to woman. I'm not even entirely sure you're the *second*-best-looking male in this household. Fact two: you are, willy-nilly, my guest. I am prepared to give you free room, board, and access to my womanly charms, in exchange for which I shall expect an average amount of respect, a bit of help with the dishes, and a chance to decide whether this little experiment is worth the trouble. Does that seem to be more or less acceptable to you, Mr. Bloom?"

"More or less."

"Fine," said the lady, "just fine. That will be more or less all for now, then." She turned on her heel and marched stiffly out of the john.

And then I realized the true nature of her invitation to stay. There was no longer any doubt about it. This was not love, this was war.

# 5

At a fashionable eight P.M., the members of our jolly *ménage à quatre* began to assemble in the dining room. I arrived first with the silverware, set three places on the table and one on the floor, and sat down with a copy of *Family Circle*. A few moments later, Harry strolled in with a copy of *Popular Mechanics*, nodded to me and sat down on the other side of the table. Then Albert padded in with a copy of *Variety*, nodded to me, settled himself on the floor next to his silverware, opened his paper and began to read.

I watched Albert carefully for five full minutes. His eyes were going back and forth on the page, but not from left to right. I knew he was faking.

"Albert," I called gently, "I know your secret."

He looked quickly up at me, ready to deny anything.

"What is the point?" I said. "Why try to be someone other than yourself? Albert," I whispered, "do you place so low a value on your own identity?"

He looked away, but I knew that my words had struck home.

"Every being on this earth was put here for a purpose, Albert. Every being has an important role to perform in life, and I defy anyone to prove that one role is any more important than any other. You see, Albert, all roles in a society are interdependent. All depend upon the roles of others for their very existence. The ruler cannot perform the role of ruler unless others are willing to perform the role of the ruled. The judge cannot perform the role of judge unless others are willing to be judged. Genet, of course, makes the same point in *The Balcony*—did you see the play when it was in town?"

Albert did not reply. Perhaps he had only seen the movie.

"Well, no matter. The movie retains his point of view. And I scarcely think that one could see it and not come away with an increased awareness of one's own importance in the greater social structure. But perhaps your problem is less in the realm of sociology than in the realm of individual psychology. Perhaps your worry is not 'What is the importance of the role of dog in the world of man?'—perhaps your worry is 'What is the effectiveness of Albert in the role of dog?' Is that it? Is that a bit closer to the truth?"

Albert looked at me briefly, then returned to *Variety*.

"Wait a moment," I said. "Don't turn away from me. Your turning away only serves to validate my hypothesis."

Albert kept validating.

"Well," I said, "so that *is* your problem. You fear that you have not been successful in performing your *normal* role expectations, and you must therefore attempt to master unusual and much more *difficult* ones in order to compensate. No mere fetcher of newspapers, you—but a reader as well."

I clucked my tongue in sympathy. "Ah, Albert, that way lies madness. Stop while you still can. Oh, you may learn to read in time—I'm not saying you won't for you are not old and it is said that only *old* dogs cannot learn new tricks—but will even that be enough for you? Won't you then fall prey to anxieties about *what* you are reading? Will you not suspect in time that you are reading below your level—that you are cheating yourself by reading only escapist literature? Will you not begin to dip into the more serious works —the classics—only to discover that the more you begin to know, the more you begin to know you *don't* know? Retreat, Albert. Come off it before it's too late. There will never be enough time to do the thing justice, and you will die an old and embittered dog."

"What kind of ideas are you putting into that animal's head?" said Bernice, entering with arms full of egg roll and gefüllte fish. "If he wants to read, let him read. You don't get old and embittered reading *Variety* unless you're in the industry, which Albert is not."

"Oh, hi, Bernice," I said. "Say, what's that delectable aroma wafting out of yon kitchen?"

"The handle of the coffeepot got a little too close to the fire." She deposited the food and disappeared back into the kitchen.

Albert came over and snuffled the gefüllte fish.

Harry stabbed an egg roll and began to chew crunch-ily.

Bernice returned with the main course.

"Surprise," she said, "lasagna au gratin. What does everybody want to drink? Harry?"

"Milk."

"Milk it shall be. Albert?"

"Whuff."

"Whuff coming up. Oliver?"

"I see I'm number three again."

"Shut up. What do you want with your meal?"

"Scintillating conversation and good cheer."

"To *drink*, smart guy. I haven't got all day."

"What have you got?"

"Coffee, tea, milk and whuff."

"Coffee, then. With."

"With what?"

"Fish."

She returned to the kitchen to mix drinks and spray Sweet-Aire.


Except for one brief, moist interlude when Albert decided to sit at the table with the rest of the grownups, the meal was not memorable. Scintillating conversation and good cheer were at a fairly low ebb, Harry hardly contributing more than Albert.

After supper, Harry washed and I dried while Bernice and Albert romped on the rug. I had still not decided on the most appropriate tone to use in communicating with Harry, so I restricted my conversation to remarks like "Where's this go, in the cupboard?" and "You finished with all the plates yet?" And Harry restricted his conversation in turn to things like "Yep" or "Nope" or "Still one plate left."

When the dishes had all been washed, dried and put away, Harry and I returned to Bernice and Albert and halfheartedly joined in the romp on the rug. I don't know whether you have ever participated in any halfhearted romps, but I can assure you that they are a good deal more tiring than the wholehearted variety since so much extra effort is involved in feigning enthusasim. By eleven, both Harry and I were all romped out. Bernice and Albert were still going pretty strong.

I felt reasonably sure that Harry had been apprised of my new role in the household, but my innate sense of discretion decreed that I wait for some sort of official announcement from Bernice before retiring to one of the Baby beds.

Harry, too, seemed to be waiting for such an edict, because instead of going to bed he lay down under the comparative safety of the television set and dozed.

Along about one in the morning, Bernice decided she had had enough.

"O.K., group," she said stretching, "time for beddy-bye."

I rose expectantly.

Bernice walked over to the television set and prodded Harry with her toe.

"Beddy-bye, Harry," she said.

Harry crawled out and stood up sleepily. Bernice grabbed him by the arm and steered him out of the room.

"Hey," I said. "Bernice?"

"Just a sec, Hare," she said and came back in to me. "Yes, Oll?"

"What gives? I thought you were sleeping with *me*."

"Well, who says I'm *not*? All I'm doing is making up Harry's bed and tucking him in. You go in and get washed up and everything. I'll be in in a second. Maybe two."

"Well . . . all right," I growled. "But you better hurry or I'll go ahead and start without you."

"Just get ready. I'll be right in. Now say good night to Harry and Albert."

"Good night, Harry and Albert."

"G'night."

"Albert, say good night to Harry and Oliver."

Albert trotted over to Harry, licked his hand, trotted over to me, licked *my* hand, and then began to nibble at my fingers.

"That's enough, Albert. Come on, Harry," and she was gone.

I shuffled into the master bedroom, lit the light on the night table, pulled back the covers on the bed and lay down without undressing. I clasped my hands behind my head. I closed my eyes. I began to wait.

When I opened my eyes, the bedside lamp was still on, I was still fully dressed, it was light outside, and Bernice was not beside me. The clock said eight thirty.

At first I was confused. Then I was amazed. Then I was enraged.

I got up and stalked into the kitchen. Bernice was merrily sectioning grapefruit.

"Morning, Oliver," she said. "Sleep well?"

"Did *you?*" My voice dripped venom.

"So-so."

"Maybe I didn't quite grasp the subtleties of our last conversation," I said, "but my understanding was that you were to be *my* guest last evening."

Bernice squirted herself in the eye with grapefruit and winced, whether from juice or me I couldn't immediately ascertain.

"Well, I mean that's what *I* figured too, Oliver. Only Harry insisted I tuck him in, and then he wanted a little huggy-bear, and one thing kind of led to another. You know how it is."

49

"I do *now*, at any rate."

"Oh, come off it, Oliver. So I didn't sleep with you last night. Big deal. So I let my husband make love to me. Is that a crime? If it's any consolation, I didn't enjoy it. Harry is still a lousy lover."

I turned to go.

"If you want to know the truth," she said, "I didn't sleep with Harry either. I slept on the living room couch." She studied the carcass of the grapefruit she had just maimed. "If you want to know the truth, I was *scared* to sleep with you."

"Scared?"

"Scared because with you I want it to be more than it was with Harry."

If you want to know the truth, I am a sucker for any sentence which begins "If you want to know the truth."

# 6

Poverty and living hand to mouth are fairly heady
things to a young middle-class painter fresh out of grad-
uate school, and if I wasn't ever able to really and truly
believe in them it was because for me they weren't ever
really and truly believable. No matter how sloppily I
dressed or how infrequently I shaved, I was conscious
of being a fraud. I have never really felt comfortable in
sloppy clothes and I have never gotten beyond the itchy

stage in beard-growing. Once I managed not to shave for three months. But there was not a single day in that entire period that I did not think, "Well, I haven't shaved it off yet," and proceed to figure out to the hour exactly how long it had been since a razor had last touched my cheek.

Perhaps some day I'll publish a Treasury of Beard Jokes. There is something about a beard that demands a commentary, it seems, even from strangers on the street. Why, I don't know. Perhaps beards are a reproof to the beardless.

In any case, I finally shaved it off and was astonished to find out what a really pleasant-looking fellow I was underneath. If for no other reason than being able to shave and rediscover one's own pleasant and dimly re-membered face underneath the stubble, I would strongly recommend the growing of a beard.

But itchiness was not the only reason that I felt a fraud in my calculated poverty. The real trouble was in my right hand: from wrist to tips of fingers it was solid fourteen karat gold. Since the beginning of art school, everything I'd ever painted was snatched from my fin-gers while the paint was still fresh and sold before it had become more than tacky.

Don't get me wrong—I am not trying in any way to pass myself off as a young Raphael—far from it. I would say that I maintain an over-all level of general unin-spired competence, and I only occasionally produce a canvas that has an ounce or two of insight. But for some curious reason, my work unhinges the brains of the sort of nice old ladies who collect portraits of children and puppydogs and pussycats with immense liquid eyes.

There are three other direct consequences of this rather mixed blessing of mine. The first is that I don't own a single piece of my own artwork. The second is that I have never known the bittersweet adventure of at least potential starvation. And the third is that I have long since sickened of painting.

The only thing I really want to be when I grow up is an art director in an advertising agency, although one of the brightest men in that profession once said advertising is no business for grown men.

In the three or four years since grad school, I have done little to attain the position of grown or ungrown ad man, spending the greater part of my time reading, lying on the beach, not chasing girls, and, every couple of months, getting out the canvas and oil paints and holding back the retch with my teeth while painting enough liquid-eyed masterpieces to cover rent, beer and TV dinners. Now, living with Bernice, even *that* bi-monthly contact with reality was spared me, and the idle life had suddenly become more than I could bear. I realized that there was nothing left to do but find an honest job.

And so, an hour or so after Bernice had confessed to me the real reason she had hesitated to share my—or, rather, *her*—bed, I was thumbing through the yellow pages in the A's looking for my first job in advertising. And an hour after that, I was walking up Hollywood Boulevard in a small suit and a large hurry, anxious to be on time for an appointment I'd made only in my mind.

The agency I was headed for occupied the penthouse suite of a giant seven-story skyscraper near the intersection of Hollywood and Vine. When I got into the elevator I pressed the button marked seven, but for some unaccountable reason the elevator stopped at the fifth floor. I was just about to not get out when a ten-foot-tall lady beckoned to me from afar with a bare bosom. I got out at five, and the elevator went on to seven alone.

The ten-foot-tall lady with the bare bosom turned out to be a giant reproduction of a girlie magazine cover, and the fifth floor turned out to be the editorial and promotional offices of *Hayday Magazine*. Below the lady with the uncovered bosom was a large desk, and behind the desk was a lady with a covered bosom. And glasses.

"May I help you?" said the covered lady.

"Yes," I said, studying the uncovered one.

"Whom did you wish to see?"

I couldn't think of an immediate reply, so she helpfully repeated the question. I saw I was being pressured into some kind of answer.

"Uh . . . is this *Hayday Magazine?*" I said, hoping to suggest by my tone of voice that I'd noticed something which made me suspect it wasn't.

"That's right. Whom did you wish to see?"

"The . . . editor. Is he in?"

"Do you have an appointment?"

"Why no. No. No, I don't, as a matter of fact. No. I

don't have an appointment, not in the conventional sense of the word," I said, still stalling for time, "but I believe that I . . . uh . . . am expected."

"What is the name, please?"

"Just say Bloom . . . is here with the . . . truth."

"Bloom . . . is here with the *truth?*"

She looked under my arm to see where I might be carrying it.

"Yes, that's . . . right," I said. "Just tell him that. He'll know."

The lady looked at me with more than routine interest, punched a button on the phone in front of her and said into the receiver: "Mr. Landsdown . . . *Bloom* is here . . . with the *truth.*"

There was a pause, during which she was doubtlessly invited to repeat the message, which she did in about the same trancelike tone I had used to deliver it. She replaced the receiver on the hook.

"Mr. Landsdown will see you," she said. I don't know which of us was more surprised.

I opened the door to Landsdown's office, walked in and closed it behind me. He didn't bother to rise. He was a big man of maybe fifty with a deeply lined face and a very close-cropped head. When he spoke it was very loud, very slow, and very bass.

"Are you Bloom?"

"Yes," I said, still in my trance.

"What is . . . the truth?"

"The truth is," I swallowed dryly, "that I need a job."

55

He considered this soberly for perhaps twenty seconds, and then exploded with laughter. His laugh was the strangest laugh I have ever heard or seen: it was a succession of very distinct ha-ha's and he never smiled once. At first I thought he was being sarcastic, but when I saw how long it was lasting, I began to relax. The laughter stopped as suddenly as it had started.

"What makes you think there *is* a job here, Bloom?"

"I don't know. Is there?"

"No."

"Oh," I said.

There didn't seem to be anything leading away from the no, so I turned and prepared to leave.

"Where are you going?" he said.

"Oh. Well, I don't know. I was just going."

"The interview isn't over. Sit down."

I sat down.

"What kind of job are you looking for?" he said.

"Art director."

"What magazines have you worked for?"

"None."

"What experience, if any, have you had in publishing?"

"None."

"Do you have any knowledge whatever about our type of operation?"

"Well, I don't really know anything about sex, but I know what I like."

"Good," he said. "What have you been doing for the last few years?"

"Mainly reading, lying on the beach, and stuff like that."

"How do you earn a living?"

"I occasionally paint children and puppydogs and pussycats with large liquid eyes."

"How did you happen to come to *Hayday?*"

"I got off at the wrong floor by mistake."

"Where were you going?"

"Up to seven. I was going to get a job in advertising."

"Why?"

"Because I'm sick of painting."

He paused and made thinking noises.

"Do you like girls?" he said.

"Yeah. Do you?"

"Don't be rude," he said, "I asked that for a very good reason. I get fifty guys in here a week wanting to work on the magazine. There seems to be a general feeling that working on a girlie magazine is one huge orgy. Well, it's not. It's a very serious business, and it's a hell of a lot of work. I put in seventy or eighty hours a week, and so does everybody else. Do you see naked women here? Of course you do. But you see so many that the novelty wears off in the first week. By the second week, you're paying more attention to the ones with the clothes. Ever been to a nudist colony?"

"Nope."

"Most boring place in the world. No mystery. Nothing left to the imagination. Nudist colony is the most puritanical society you'll ever see."

He stopped and made thinking noises again.

"Still want to work here?" he said.

I shrugged.

"I thought you said there was no job open," I said.

"I did. I changed my mind. You seem to have at least average intelligence, and I like your candor. There's plenty to be done here if you're willing to do it. How much are you asking?"

"Five hundred a month."

He massaged his jaw.

"What do you think you've got that entitles you to a salary like that?" he said.

"At least average intelligence, and no previous experience to muddle my thinking."

He continued to massage his jaw.

"We'll try it for a week," he said, "and then we'll see what we'll see. You start tomorrow. Be here at nine sharp. If you're late, you're fired. Good day, Bloom."

"Good day, Landsdown," I said and left.

I got into the elevator and started to push the button marked one. Then I did a curious thing. I pushed the button marked seven instead. When the doors opened I checked the far wall. Where the ten-foot-tall lady had been on the fifth floor, there was only a name on the seventh. It said "Plapert, Kernig, Carston & Robbins." The lady behind the desk was small, blonde, and prerecorded.

"Welcome to Plapert, Kernig, Carston and Robbins," she said. "Whom did you wish to see?"

I looked up at the wall.

"Plapert," I said.

"I'm sorry, Mr. Plapert is not in at present. Is there someone else who can help you?"

"Kernig," I said.

"I'm sorry, Mr. Kernig is not in at present. Is there someone else who can help you?"

"Carston," I said.

"I'm sorry, Mr. Carston is not in at present. Is there someone else who can help you?"

I stared at her very steadily.

"No," I said, "I'm afraid there isn't."

"Would you like to speak with Mr. Robbins?"

"Is he in?" I said warily.

"Yes."

"O.K. then, I'll speak to Robbins."

"I'm sorry, Mr. Robbins is in conference," she said.

I came up very close to the desk and placed my face two inches away from hers.

"Tell Robbins I wish to speak to him," I said through clenched teeth.

"I'm sorry, Mr. Rob—"

"*Tell* him."

"Very well. Did you have an appointment?"

"TELL HIM."

"Wh-whom shall I say is calling?"

"Tell him *Bloom* is here . . . with the truth."

"*Bloom* is here . . . with the truth?"

"That's right."

"Very well."

She punched a button on the phone and spoke into the receiver.

**59**

"Mr. Robbins, a Mr. Bloom says he is here with . . . the truth." Pause. "Bloom." Pause. "Truth." Pause. "Yes, Mr. Robbins."

The lady put the receiver back and looked up at me. "Fourth door on your left," she said.

I tweaked her nose and went in search of Robbins.

When I opened the door, Robbins was seated behind a desk, his back toward me, looking out the window at Hollywood Boulevard. Although I couldn't see one, it looked like he was smoking a pipe.

"Robbins?" I said.

"Come in, come in," he said through the pipestem. "Sit down, sit down."

"Thank you, thank you," I said and sat.

"Bloom, is it?"

"Yes."

"Receptionist said you're here with the truth."

"Yes."

"Good. Good. Precious little of it left in this business, God knows."

"Yes."

He had given me the wrong straight line and now I was stuck. I decided to try anyway.

"The truth is," I said, "I need a job."

He didn't react at all, not even after a suitable twenty second delay. I was afraid he hadn't heard me.

"The truth is," I said a little more loudly, "I need a job."

"I heard you, I heard you. I'm not deaf, you know."

60

"Sorry," I said.

He continued to puff at his pipe and study Hollywood Boulevard.

"See those people?" he said at last.

"Where?" I said.

"Down there. Hollywood Boulevard."

"Oh. Yes?"

"That's your market. That's who you're trying to sell. You don't sell *them*, you don't sell the product. Remember that."

"O.K.," I said.

"Study them," he said. "Study them till you know them better than you know yourself."

"O.K.," I said.

"That's the only way to do good advertising. That's the *only* way to do good advertising."

"O.K.," I said.

"What are you—copywriter?"

"No," I said. "Art director."

He sucked his pipe and continued to do good advertising on Hollywood Boulevard.

"We need a copywriter," he said.

"I see."

"Like to do some copywriting?"

"Sure."

"What experience have you had?"

"What—in copywriting, you mean?"

"Yes."

"Why, none," I said. "I'm an art director."

"Then why are you applying for a copy job?"

I gave this a lot of thought.

"Well," I said, "I've been down on Hollywood Boulevard a long, long time and I think I know those people better than I know myself. So what's the difference whether I do art or copy—I know how to sell *people*."

"*I'd* say so, at any rate," he said at any rate. "How much money you need?"

"Five hundred to start," I said, "and a substantial raise in six months. Also all fringe benefits, including hospitalization, major medical, profit sharing plan, retirement fund and use of the company parking lot."

"Fair enough," he said, "assuming you're still *here* in six months. O.K., you can start tomorrow at nine. Or nine-thirty. Or whenever you want. But don't get the wrong idea. This is a serious business, and it's a hell of a lot of work. So long, Bloom."

"So long, Robbins," I said.

He never turned around.

In the first floor lobby was a public phone booth. I entered, deposited a dime in the slot and prepared to dial. On a whim I hung up, walked over to the candy counter and got a dollar's worth of nickels. In the men's room I washed and dried the nickels, then returned to the phone booth. I put two nickels in the slot, the rest of them in my mouth, and dialed.

"Hello?"

"Hello," I said through a herd of buffalo. "Is this Bernice Baby?"

"Hello—yes, this is she."

"Thank God."

"What? Hello?"

"Hello, Mrs. Baby, I am vastly relieved. Vastly. I feared for a moment that you would not be home. The purpose of my call, you see, is to ask you to be my wife."

"To whom am I speaking, please?"

"My name is Blumberg. Aristotle Blumberg. A likable, medium-salaried man in his middle forties. Nice gray eyes. Good strong bones and teeth. Aristotle Blumberg. First say you'll marry me, then we'll talk."

"I think maybe we've got a lousy connection. You sound like you got a mouth full of nickels."

I removed about half of the nickels and continued.

"I said my name is Aristotle Blumberg and I've asked for your hand in marriage."

"Who is this, *Oliver?*"

"Blumberg. This is Aristotle Blumberg."

"Blumberg. I don't know anybody named Blumberg."

"No, of course not. But we do have the same laundryman. I saw your name on a laundry list. Bernice Baby, it said. Instantly I went limp. Who is that Bernice Baby, I asked the laundryman. A lady, he said—a nice lady with a dimpled chin, a wistful smile, and candy-striped sheets. Has she a husband, I said. No, he said, it's a widow lady. In that case, I said, I shall have to ask her to be my wife."

"Are you having a little fun at my expense, Mr. Blumberg?"

63

"Not in the least. To the contrary, my dear lady. I'm so serious it frightens me half to death. It's not every day I ask a lady to be my wife."

"Of course not. I'm sure you're a very discriminating-type fella."

"I shall ignore the possible ironic observation and let it roll quickly and easily over my back. Mrs. Baby—I shall call you Mrs. Baby prior to the wedding ceremony, owing to the fact that we have not as yet been formally introduced—Mrs. Baby, I must tell you that there is a certain poetry in your name."

"Listen, Blumberg, I got a sink full of dishes and I'm up to my armpits in Joy. You got something serious to say, say it. I don't have all day."

"Another peppy remark. Well, why not—a woman should not be a dishrag. A little spunk is perfectly acceptable. Mrs. Baby, I shall be candid. I am a relatively lonely man. I live by myself in an efficiency kitchen with a twenty-seven-inch television, a nice Simmons Hide-a-Bed, and an elderly Yorkshire Terrier who snores.

"Each morning at precisely six-forty-five, I awake, stand up, dress, brush my teeth and open up two cans of tunafish—one for me and one for the elderly Yorkshire Terrier. We eat, I wash the dishes, have one cup of coffee, no cream or sugar, and hide the Simmons. At precisely seven-twenty-eight I run out of the apartment, scramble nimbly down the stairs, and catch the seven-thirty Olympic Boulevard bus at a dead run. All day long I total up stacks of figures on a secondhand adding machine. Sometimes I have a cigarette with a fellow, Arthur Mandelbaum, who has the next desk, sometimes I don't. Promptly at four-fifteen, I run out of the office, race quickly down three flights of stairs and catch the same Olympic Boulevard bus back to my apartment.

"Supper is out of a can or in a frozen aluminum tray with tiny compartments for peas, mashed potatoes and some form of chopped meat. Occasionally there is a peppy slogan on the wrapper like 'Heat in a 450° (hot) oven for twenty-five minutes, remove, and enjoy piping hot.' With me it is never piping hot. Occasionally scalding. Occasionally lukewarm, when I turn off the oven and become absorbed in a program on the television. Then I feed the Yorkshire, make up the Simmons, and climb into bed.

"That is my life, Mrs. Baby. It is not a bad life, but every so often I wish it were otherwise. When I saw your name on the laundry list, I knew it was a sign from Above."

"You would like to be married, Mr. Blumberg?"

"I would like to be married."

"Then please get married and do not call strange women on the telephone and ask them to be your wife just because you see their name on a laundry list."

"I shall pretend not to notice the rude and unfriendly tone provoked by my sincere and honorable request."

There was a brief silence.

"How can you possibly propose marriage to someone you know nothing about?"

"Dear lady, I smile at your sincere but misguided question. First, it is not true that I know nothing about you. I know you have a dimpled chin, a wistful smile, and candy-striped sheets. I know that you are a widow lady. And I know that you are Bernice Baby.

"Second, in other countries—and even in this one not so very long ago—a marriage between a man and a lady would be arranged without so much as a telephone call between the parties in question. And most of those marriages, my dear Mrs. Baby, turned out very nicely indeed. No divorces, no running away to Reno with the children, and"—I paused for emphasis—"no separate bedrooms either. After a wedding is plenty of time to get acquainted. Thirdly, assuming I changed my mind upon meeting you, it would still not be too late to call off the wedding. A breach of promise suit based on a telephone call between two strangers would not remain very long in the courts. So we go into this thing with our eyes wide open—eh, Mrs. Baby? Now then, what do you say?"

I did not like the quality of silence on the other end of the line.

"Mrs. Baby?"

Still more silence.

"Bernice?"

All I could hear was regular breathing. I took the rest of the nickels out of my mouth.

"Bernice," I said softly, "it's Oliver."

More breathing, not so regular. There were no sobs, but I thought I heard a tear thud to the floor.

"Bernice, honey, I'm sorry. It was supposed to be a joke. It was supposed to make you laugh."

Now I heard the sobs. I felt really rotten.

"Bernice, listen. Can you hear me? Are you listening? Bernice? Listen, honey, I'm sorry. I swear to God I was just joking. I thought you'd get a kick out of it. I called to tell you good news. That I got a job. That I got *two* jobs. That I'm earning a thousand dollars a month. Bernice? Can you hear me? I'm sorry, sweetheart. Old Oliver just stepped on his floppy old tongue again, that's all. A little tomfoolery in terrible taste. I am really, really sorry. I swear to God. I feel rotten, Bernice, really rotten. Please forgive me, will you? Honey? Will you?"

Someone blew their nose noisily into the telephone.

"All right. Come home, Oliver." Another good snort. "I'll fix you a nice home-cooked supper—not from a frozen aluminum tray and with no peppy slogans. But no more talk of marriage."

"O.K., sweetheart, O.K. I'll be there in about twenty minutes. I'll take a cab. I really am sorry. O.K.?"

"O.K."

"O.K."

# 7

Supper that night did not differ appreciably from the night before. I still set the table and the floor, Harry still read *Popular Mechanics,* and Albert still struggled with *Variety.* The scintillation level of our mealtime conversation had not risen.

The after-dinner chores remained approximately the same—Harry washing, me drying, Bernice and Albert romping. As before, Harry crawled under the television at eleven and, as before, Bernice dragged him out again at one. But once she had coached everybody in their exit lines and was about to depart with Harry for the tucking-in ceremonies, I caught her by the wrist and whispered harshly in her ear:

"Where are you going?"

"To tuck Harry in."

"And *then* where?"

"To tuck Albert in."

"And *then* where?"

"To bed with you."

"How do you expect me to trust you after what happened last night?"

"I don't actually see that you have any alternative."

I didn't care for her response, but she was right. So, as before, I went sulking into the master bedroom, lit the light on the night table, pulled back the covers on the bed, lay down without undressing, clasped my hands behind my head, closed my eyes and began to wait.

When I opened my eyes, the bedside lamp was still lit, I was still fully dressed, it was still dark outside, and Bernice was standing at the foot of the bed.

"Hey," I said. "You came back after all."

"I suppose so," she said.

"Come here. Sit down."

"In a minute."

A minute passed. She remained standing.

"Bernice?"

"Yes?"

70

"Are you still afraid?"

"I suppose so," she said.

I got to my feet and took her in my arms.

"Don't be afraid," I said. "We're going to do nice things. It will be very pleasant."

"O.K.," she said.

She let me kiss her. She let me slip off her dress. She let me slip off her slip. She let me bring her down on the bed and smooth her out on the sheets. She let me slip off the rest of her underthings. Her body was soft and warm and soapy smelling. But Bernice was not inside of it.

"Bernice," I whispered.

"Yes?"

"Where are you?"

"I don't know."

"Are you with Harry?"

Pause.

"No."

"Where are you?"

"I don't know."

"Bernice, I want to make love to you."

"Yes."

"But only if you can be present to enjoy it. I don't want to make love to a proxy."

"O.K."

"Does that seem fair?"

"I suppose so."

"Does it?"

"Yes."

71

"Can you come back from wherever you are?"

Pause.

"I don't think so."

I pulled slightly away and studied her.

"Does it have something to do with Harry?"

Pause.

"Partly."

"Do you love Harry?"

Pause.

"I don't think so."

"Do you feel guilty about Harry?"

"Partly."

"Do you . . . want me to make love to you?"

Pause.

"I think so."

"But not with Harry here?"

"Maybe not."

"Can't you ask him to leave?"

"No."

"Can't you ask him for a divorce?"

"No."

"Why not?"

"I just can't."

"Why not?"

"Just because."

"Just because *what?*"

She turned her head away from me. I turned it back.

"Just because *what*, Bernice?"

"Just because, for one thing, I happen to know what it feels like to be hurt."

72

"You think you'd hurt Harry if you asked him for a divorce?"

"I don't think. I know."

"You think Harry is in love with you."

"In his own way he is, yes. In his own way, Harry is very much in love with me. In my own way, as long as we're on the subject, I am also in love with him."

I placed the flat of my hand on her forehead.

"Is this where you love him, Bernice?"

"I don't know what you mean."

I placed my hand on the soft flesh of her breast, over her heart.

"Is this where you love him?" I said.

Pause.

"I don't know." Softer.

I placed my hand on her warm belly.

"Is this where?"

"I don't know." Softer yet.

I slid the belly hand around to the small of her back and pulled her in against my body.

"Where do you love him. Bernice?" I whispered. "With what part of you do you love him? Not with your head—not with your heart—not with your belly—so with what do you love him, Bernice?"

I hugged her hard, lust beginning to fill up my throat. I rubbed my face along her skin. I kissed. I licked. I nipped. I chewed. I started to sink in a warm black sea and the waters closed over my head. I sank and sank and the deeper I sank the greater grew the cubic pounds of pressure inside my body and out. I had the bends. I had to breathe. I couldn't. And, drowning, I felt a sob beginning at the base of my spine, spreading outwards and upwards, convulsing my lungs, paralyzing my limbs, compressing an entire ocean into a tumbler of water and suddenly sucking it out through a pinhole.

I lay limp, emptied, drenched in sweat, gulping air.

"Bernice," I said between gulps. "Love. Love me."

She said something into the pillow that I couldn't make out.

"What, darling?" I said, "I can't hear you."

Gently I turned her head.

"I don't love anybody," she said.

I sank back into the bed. I was too spent to react. I really was. I was too tired to even allow a sound wave to vibrate my eardrum.

"I don't love anybody at all," she said.

"All right."

"I don't. Not you, not Harry, not anybody."

"All right."

"Not even me."

"All right. Sleep first, we'll destroy each other later."

"*Especially* not me, as a matter of fact."

"All right."

"Listen," she said in a new tone. "What did we just do?"

"Huh?"

"What did we just do?"

"Uh . . . what?"

"Did we just commit adultery?"

74

"Look, I'm very tired, Bernice—"

"Did we? I think we did. We just committed adultery. I've never done that before. That's a pretty serious thing, adultery, isn't it? A sin, or something. I don't think I even enjoyed it. I think it's kind of sad to do something as serious as adultery and not even enjoy it. I wasn't even—how do they say it—aroused? I wasn't even aroused. Hey, I thought you said you didn't want to make love to me if I couldn't be present to enjoy it. I thought you said you didn't want to make love to a proxy. Wasn't that what you said? I thought that was what you said. Wasn't it?"

"Yes."

"So how come you changed your mind? How come you decided to go ahead without me, huh?"

"Lay off, Bernice," I whispered. "Please."

"First tell me how come you changed your mind."

Sigh.

"I guess I just got carried away. I'm sorry."

"You're *sorry*. Oh, well, if you're *sorry* then it's all right. If you're sorry then we'll just forget it ever happened.

Quietly: "Were you raped, Bernice?"

"What?"

"Were you raped? Do you want to press charges? Because if you do, I want to hear how you do it." Falsetto: "You see, officer, I was lying naked in bed with this person who lives with us and we were having this very interesting philosophical discussion and everything, when, suddenly, he rapes me."

"Very funny," she said.

"Is that about the way it happened, Mrs. Baby? We'd like to get the details straight for the official complaint. Would you say that was about the way it happened?"

She pondered her fingernails.

"O.K., Bernice, I think I've made my point. Now then. Would you prefer that I pack up and leave right now, or may we postpone our adieus until the morning?"

She inhaled, narrowed her eyes, and gave me a level look.

"You so much as *try* to leave this house, my friend— now, tomorrow, next week, or anytime before I decide I'm ready to let you go—and I will feed you personally and very slowly to my large dog for his breakfast." She got out of bed and gathered up her clothes. "And that," she said, "is a solemn promise."

# 8

Maybe it was that I had nowhere else to go. Maybe it was that I was not yet so involved with Bernice that I had to walk out on her. Maybe it was just that I'd chosen not to end my days as Albert's breakfast. Whatever the reason, at eight-thirty the next morning, I climbed into Bernice's Morris Minor and began to drive rapidly toward Hollywood and Vine.

At nine sharp I entered the fifth-floor offices of *Hay-*

*day Magazine* and began my career in art direction, the first hour of which was devoted to a lecture by Landsdown on the seriousness of the girlie magazine business. When he finished, I mumbled something about a coffee break, excused myself, and took the elevator up to seven.

At ten sharp I entered the seventh-floor offices of Plapert, Kernig, Carston & Robbins and began my career in copywriting—the first hour of which was devoted to a lecture by Robbins on the seriousness of the ad game. When he finished, I murmured "coffee break" again and returned to the fifth floor.

From eleven till twelve noon I labored in the serious world of girlie art. Then I stretched, said "lunchtime," and went back upstairs to the serious world of advertising.

From noon to one-thirty I pounded my seventh-floor typewriter. Then I stretched, said "lunchtime" again, and descended once more to my fifth-floor drawing board.

For the next hour and a half I drew. At three o'clock I announced "coffee time" and rang for the elevator.

For the following hour I typed. At four o'clock I heralded another coffee hour and got back in the elevator.

I really bore down and directed art with a vengeance for the next sixty minutes. Then, at five, I yawned, allowed as how it was time to go home, and took the elevator back upstairs.

From five to six I advertised like crazy. And at six

o'clock Robbins personally came into my office to suggest I knock off for the day.

"No need to overdo it, Bloom," he said through his pipestem. "Seems to me you've put in a pretty good day's work."

"You hardly know the half of it, sir," I said.

Except for the hour lecture by Robbins, I had spent my first day of copywriting at the typewriter, trying to look efficient. Since Robbins hadn't given me any accounts to work on as yet, I had to content myself with variations on the popular themes of good men coming to the aid of their parties and quick brown foxes jumping over lazy dogs. By six o'clock I had accrued several sheaves of each.

Similarly, since Landsdown had limited the discussion of my occupational duties to the purely theoretical, the drawings I turned out in my alternate hours at the magazine were essentially busywork drawings and had no immediate practical value, unless *Hayday* were to consider publishing a portfolio of sketches featuring ladies and puppydogs with large liquid eyes, in decidedly compromising situations.

It is said that no man can serve two masters. A more accurate observation might be that no man can serve two masters and still find time for lunch. Because, in my tightly scheduled day, a real lunch hour was the one item I had not succeeded in programing.

79

Other than that, I was rather proud of the way I had managed, especially since my alternate-houred time-table had been as spontaneous as my decision to take the second job in the first place. I had no idea, by the end of the first day of work, how long I could continue this dual allegiance, but I was more or less committed to finding out.

Were Albert a more outspoken polemicist, he could have taken the judgment I had leveled against him and thrown it back in my teeth: I had accused him of over-compensation in his attempt to read as well as fetch a newspaper. Couldn't he accuse me of overcompensation too? Wasn't the holding of *both* jobs a ready-made alibi for failure in either?

Well, if Albert was shrewd enough to challenge me, I had a convincing rebuttal. I did not fear failure in either job for two very good reasons:

First, I had acquainted both employers with my lack of experience. And second, I am a devout believer in Bloom's Law of Universal Incompetence.

Bloom's Law of Universal Incompetence states: *No matter how lousy you are at any given job, almost everybody else is lousier.* Or, to put it a bit more accurately: The minute you learn how to perform any given job with even minimum proficiency, you are immediately better at it than a fixed and incredibly large number of people.

If this axiom seems a bit severe, it should be noted that it is based on years of careful observation in many walks of life, both academic and practical, public and private, civilian and military. And it has never failed me.

So, armed with my timetable and Bloom's Law, I felt at least moderately optimistic about my chances for success in my new chosen professions.

At six-thirty or so, I pulled the Morris Minor merrily into the driveway, hopped out, skipped across the lawn and up the steps to the house.

I unlocked the door, stepped into the hallway, and somebody in the living room—possibly Harry—said, "Hey, I heard a noise."

I closed the door softly behind me and listened.

"Hey," said Harry (for that's who it was), "did you hear a noise?"

Silence.

"Hey, Bernice," said Harry, "I think Ollie is home."

I walked quietly up to the living room doorway, peered in, and immediately took a rather large mortar shell through my stomach.

Strewn gaily about the room in wild abandon were many articles of male and female clothing: A pair of trousers straddled a coffee table. A pair of panties hung from the corner of a picture frame. A brassiere dangled rakishly from the chandelier.

In the middle of the carpet lay Harry, quite unclothed. In the middle of Harry lay Bernice, similarly attired.

"Oh, uh, hiya, Oll," said Harry, "I and Bernice here were just talking about you."

81

Harry struggled to get up, but Bernice hung on for dear life.

It wasn't that I was, as they say, rooted to the spot. It was more that I had sort of forgotten precisely who I was and what else I could otherwise have been doing at that particular moment. I was not at all nervous. In fact I don't believe I have ever been more thoroughly relaxed in my entire life. I think that a fair description of my feeling, in fact, was that I was vertically lying down.

Harry, on the other hand, was not at all relaxed.

"Listen, Oll," he said, finally shaking free of Bernice and getting to his feet, "let me fix you a drink."

Bernice decided to sit up, but otherwise remained on the floor.

"I think you'd better sit down, Oll, old man," said Harry nervously. He laid a hand on my shoulder and the shoulder seemed to give way under the weight. I was sinking slowly into the carpet, but the sensation was more that of falling lazily upward through the ceiling.

Harry grabbed me under the arms and helped me into an armchair.

"There," he said, "that's better. Now, what can I fix you? Bourbon? How's about some bourbon, Oll? Bourbon sound good to ya, ha?"

I had forgotten how tongues and voice boxes worked exactly. You tend to forget stuff like that when you're unusually relaxed.

"O.K., Oll. Bourbon coming right up, boy."

Harry ran to the liquor cabinet and took out the bottle of bourbon. He poured some into a glass.

"Hey, Oll, what do you like with it?" he said. "Ya want soda with it or ginger ale or what?"

No sound seemed likely to come from me in the foreseeable future. Harry was obviously getting very sad. I wished that I could help him, but I couldn't really think how.

"O.K., pal, ginger ale it is," said Harry. "Ginger ale coming right up."

He ran into the kitchen and opened the refrigerator.

"Oh-oh," he called, "no ginger ale. Is soda all right?"

I continued not answering.

"Oh-oh," he said, "no soda here either. Say, Oll, there doesn't seem to be anything here to mix it with. Not unless you want it with clam juice, that is." Pause. "Hey, Oll, you want to try it with clam juice?"

Harry slammed the refrigerator door and reappeared in the living room with a glass of bourbon and a bottle of clam juice. He looked at me, then at the clam juice, then back at me. He shrugged, poured some clam juice on top of the bourbon and brought it over to me.

"Here ya go, Oll," said Harry, extending the glass.

I wanted to take it from him, just to make him feel better. I really wanted to.

"Oll? Come on, Oll, have a drink. It'll make you feel like a new man."

All I could do was stare.

Harry seemed on the verge of panic.

"Hey!" he yelled. "HEY!"

He took the bourbon and the clam juice and threw it in my face.

I jumped. I was alive. I began to wipe the liquid off my face.

Harry was obviously relieved. He walked over to Bernice and pushed her with his foot.

"Hey, Bernice," he said.

Bernice was also alive. She stood up slowly and put on somebody's shirt.

"Listen, everybody," said Harry. He looked around.

You couldn't really say everybody was *listening*, but then neither could you say they *weren't*.

"I just wanted to say," he said, not at all sure what it was he wanted to say, "I just wanted to say that, uh, that we are all, uh . . . all friends. What I mean is, we are all people who are . . . people who don't want to hurt anybody or make them sad or . . . anything, but I think that maybe we, uh, can't help but keep bumping into each other and knocking each other down and hurting each other because I don't think we know . . . where we are going. I mean, I don't think any of us really know where we are going."

Bernice, who had begun to pick up clothes and put them on without much regard for whose they were, had stopped and looked now as though she might really be listening.

"That's not really what I wanted to say," said Harry. "What I meant was that we don't *care* where we are going. We don't care where anybody *else* is going, either. We don't at all. That's maybe why we keep bumping into everybody. That's maybe . . . that's maybe why . . ."

Harry stopped talking. He looked like he was beginning to feel really dumb. Embarrassed, maybe. Or scared. He looked like he didn't know what was worse —to have started talking in the first place, or to have stopped. Because the minute he stopped it was obvious he would never be able to start again.

He looked at Bernice and saw that Bernice was watching him very hard. And as he watched back, she put her arms around his naked body and she kissed his fuzzy chest.

"Harry," whispered Bernice, "will you marry me?"

Harry nodded slowly, closed his eyes, and kissed back.

Twelve minutes and eighteen seconds later, I had packed my things and left the Baby house for good.

# 9

For pure unabashed unrelenting JOY, nothing but nothing gives me a warmer inner glow than bringing two hearts who have drifted apart back together again.

Turgid with joy, I raced from the scene of my reconciliatory triumph with suitcases banging against my thighs. But, alas, so suddenly had come the fruition of my labors that I was left quite homeless, and soon found myself returning for the fifth time that day to the offices of *Hayday Magazine,* there to set up light housekeeping in the art department.

Substantial salary advances from both employers enabled me, within a week, to lease (1) a Corvette Sting Ray with authentic gas engine and (2) a Laurel Canyon cottage with authentic gas fireplace, thus thrusting me bodily into the hurly-burly of Hollywood statusdom.

I had never been aware of a desire for such overt manifestations of status, but my new needs for lodging and transportation and my new roles of adman and girlieman had cross-pollinated and developed a new and exotic Bloom. Gone forever was the wastrel painter, bearded beach bum and all-purpose ne'er-do-well. In his place stood a dedicated, smooth-shaven, neatly pressed, dual-carbureted, rustic-cottaged master of mass media. If Beach Bum Bloom wore dark glasses to protect his eyes from the glare of the sun, Mass Media Bloom wore them to protect his colleagues from the brilliance of his own ideas, shining out through his baby-browns.

Mass Media Bloom was quick to pick up all the subtleties of his new role in Western communications. I learned how to lace my conversations with phrases like "Are-you-ready-for-that?" and "You-kidding-me?" and "Dry-Beefeater-martini-with-a-twist." I learned how to speak of an enemy as "a very sweet guy with a lot of problems." I learned how to speak of a friend as "a very sweet guy with a lot of problems." I started seeing an analyst in Beverly Hills three afternoons a week.

Treatment (for that was the term one used when one referred to one's analysis) might have been difficult for me to fit into my already crowded day, were I still following my initial timetable of work. However, after little more than a week, I began to realize that even four and a half daylight hours in each office per diem was excessive. People who spent too much time in the office were suspected of not having enough to do.

I did not see Bernice again. Los Angeles is a big city —or a big conglomeration of suburbs—and I and Bernice did not exactly move in the same circles.

Once I spotted a thin lady with a big German shepherd on Hollywood Boulevard and I followed them for several blocks, operating on the rationale that I was going in that direction anyway and that it might be fun to run into Bernice and Albert and talk about old times. But the lady was not Bernice and the German shepherd was not Albert, and when I passed by and looked at them the dog growled and I growled back.

Another time I was having a party in my rustic Laurel Canyon cabin, and after a few dry-Beefeater-martinis-with-a-twist I thought it might be a nice gesture to invite Bernice and Harry up.

But nobody answered the telephone, when I called, though it did seem to me I heard faint barking sounds between the rings.

Sober, I never really considered calling. In fact, after the first few weeks of treatment, I didn't even mention Bernice to my analyst. Psychoanalytically, we had written off my stay with the Babys as the symbolic enactment of a normal childhood wish to steal my mother away from my father.

The work at *Hayday* was much as Landsdown had prophesied. I *did* start supervising shooting sessions, and the novelty of working with naked ladies *did* eventually wear thin (though it took a little longer than Landsdown estimated), but one office is pretty much like the next, once you get used to the company's product.

And then one Friday night Landsdown threw a party. He threw it in his costly home in Brentwood, and if the guests did not drive right up and park in his living room it was not because there wasn't enough space.

The guests were magnificent. They stood like an orchard of trees, heavy with the ripe fruit of droppable names. I passed among them, harvesting, breaking off a succulent surname here, a still-green given name there. My arms were almost full when I saw something that made me lose all interest in agriculture.

A thin blonde lady in a heartbreakingly outmoded gown stood in the corner nursing what appeared to be a screwdriver.

"Say," I said, striding up to her with a look of genuine fascination on my face, "that wouldn't be a screwdriver you've got there by any chance, would it?"

The thin blonde lady looked up, startled. Then she realized she was in an environment where it was permissible to speak to strangers, and that awareness, taking shape with difficulty on her face, organized her features into a smile's second cousin.

"Oh," she said, squinting up at me, "why, uh, yes. It is. Yes."

"Golly," I said, "I've heard so much about them, but I've never really tasted a real screwdriver before. May I?"

The thin blonde lady was worried. If she let me taste it, I would leave microbes on the glass, and it was not a good idea to have microbes on your glass from the mouth of a person who hadn't even been formally introduced to you. On the other hand, if she refused she might hurt my feelings.

"Oh, uh, be my guest," she said, handing me the glass, apparently deciding that she wouldn't take another sip of it if I turned out to be a bad sort of fellow.

"Why, you know," I said, smacking my lips, "it's rather good. But they put far too much vodka in it for my taste."

"They did? Oh, I mean, yes. Yes, that was what I told the gentleman who mixed it for me, as a matter of fact."

The lady squinted at my face to see if it held any clue to the presence or absence of sincerity.

"Are you having trouble with your vision, miss?" I said. "I notice that you appear to be squinting."

"Well, uh . . . as a matter of fact, I normally do wear glasses."

"You do? Why, how marvelous. Where are yours— not broken, I hope?"

"Why, no. It's just that, well, that is to say, when one attends social functions one tries to . . . look one's best, you might say, and . . ."

91

"Look one's *best?* You mean, dear lady, that you seriously believe a woman does not look her best wearing glasses?"

"Well, I only—"

"Why, I honestly believe that's what you really think."

"Well, as a matter of—"

"I don't know about other men, but, frankly, I adore glasses on a woman."

"You do?"

"Heavens, yes. It makes them look so . . . intelligent, so sensible. You know what I mean?"

"Well yes, I . . . Listen, I believe I've brought mine with me in my purse. Do you . . . I mean, shall I put them on for you?"

"Oh my. What a question. Shall I put them *on* for you, she asks. Of *course* put them on."

The lady poked around in her purse, dropped her lipstick, dropped some hairpins, dropped a box of Sen-Sen, and finally located her glasses. She took them out of their case and slipped them on. They were, thank God, not wire-rimmed.

I faked a rather theatrical double-take and placed my hands solemnly on both her shoulders.

"Why, miss," I said, "you're . . . you're beautiful."

The lady's cheeks glowed.

"Oh no," she said, lowering her eyes.

"Yes yes, I mean it. You're absolutely lovely." I took her hand in both of mine with great feeling. "As a matter of fact," I said, "now that I see the true nature of your beauty I fear that I can never hope to win your heart. Therefore"— I raised her hand to my lips—"I shall leave you now, while the vision of your lovely face is not yet deeply etched upon my memory, and with the hope that, in time, I shall be able to forget you."

I bowed, flashed her a tragic smile and, the game now complete, turned to go.

"Wait," called the lady, "My name is . . . Alice."

The name and the hopeless sincerity of its offering caught me in the kidneys like a kick. I turned around and tried the tragic smile.

"I must go, really I must."

"No, please. Stay for a moment. You needn't be afraid of me."

She held out her hand to me. Not knowing what else to do with it, I took it.

"Well," said the lady coyly, "I've told you *my* name. Now you've got to tell me yours."

"Oliver," I said.

"Oliver is a lovely name," said the lady with a strange confident tone that seemed as unfamiliar to the speaker as to her audience. "Come, let's go out on the terrace and inhale some fresh air."

It's still not too late, I thought. I can just excuse myself and disappear.

"Say, listen," I said, "I just remembered. I promised someone I'd dance with them. Old school friend. Girl I used to have a mad crush on in the eighth grade. Beautiful girl. Never dared ask her out because I figured she was so popular, you know? At dances she was always with some older man nobody knew. Turns out everybody else in the school was just as scared to ask her out as I was, and the older man was a cousin she imported from a nearby university, just to save face at school dances. Funny. She was the lonesomest girl in the school. If she had been plain-looking, the boys would've been all over her like a cold sweat. The plain ones are always more popular, it seems."

"That happens not to be the case," said the lady, her confident tone leaking out of her grasp like a fistful of sand. "It was very nice to, uh, have . . . made your acquaintance. I, uh, shan't keep you."

"No, wait," I said. I can't bear pain, especially that of others. I also happen to be a sucker for the word "shan't."

"Now that I think of it," I said, "my friend did say not before midnight, and"—glancing rapidly at my watch—"it's scarcely ten-thirty. Let's hit that terrace."

"Well . . . all right," said the lady dubiously, and allowed me to repossess her hand.

All I have to do, I reasoned as we pushed our way through the throng toward the terrace, is to restore that beautiful confident tone I heard in her voice before. Then I will be able to mount my white horse and gallop away into the distance, leaving her to ask "Who was that masked man?"

The terrace overlooked the entire San Fernando Valley. Below us, five billion tiny lights winked up from an unending constellation of heavily mortgaged pastel-stuccoed houses.

"It's beautiful," said Alice.

"Ah yes," I said, "it is."

Standing behind her, I raised my arms and tucked them around her small body. She stiffened slightly, but did not otherwise object. I bent down and placed my cheek against her neck. I counted slowly to ten and gently brushed my lips along her shoulder. She pretended not to notice. I counted to twenty-five and planted a tender kiss at the back of her neck. At the count of thirty I planted one on her cheek. At the count of thirty-five I swung her around and planted one on her mouth, except that she ducked at the last second and the corner of her glasses lacerated my lip. I stifled a yelp and shot my hand to my mouth.

"What's the matter?" she whispered.

"It's nothing," I replied, reaching for my handkerchief, "just a minor flesh wound."

"What? Let me see."

She raised herself on tiptoes and tried to peer into my mouth.

"It's O.K.," I said. "Don't worry about it."

"No, let me see, I studied medicine once. Take the handkerchief away and face the light."

I took away the handkerchief, faced the light and let her look.

"Oh, it's not so terrible," she laughed. "It's not even bleeding."

"Well," I said in my best wounded tone, "then I guess it doesn't hurt."

"Does it hurt?"

95

"I guess not."

"No, does it?"

"Not if it's not supposed to."

"Oh, come on, Oliver. Tell me. Does it really hurt?"

"A little."

"Oh, I *am* sorry. I really am. It's these darn glasses. Wasn't it the glasses?"

"I don't know."

"It was. It was the glasses. Darn things—I knew I shouldn't have put them on."

She took them off and put them in her purse.

"All I wanted was one lousy kiss."

"I know. I'm sorry. I don't know why I did that." She put her hand on my cheek. "Here," she said, obviously deciding that such a nice fellow couldn't possibly have dangerous microbes, and gave me a quick peck on the mouth. "Does that feel better now?"

The instinctive doctor-mother in every woman: kissing a hurt to make it feel better.

"I don't know."

"How about this?" Another kiss. "Does *that* feel better?"

Kissing it to make it feel better: the single greatest medical discovery in five thousand years, and ignored by the entire medical profession. ("What, nurse, you say he's not responding to declomycin? Well, we've still got one thing left in our bag of tricks. Gentlemen, has any of you tried kissing it to make it feel better?")

"That," I said, "makes it feel a *little* better. But one more ought to really heal it up."

She kissed me again, and I was able to part her lips with my tongue.

"How was that?" she said, a little out of breath.

"Healed without a scar."

"Good." She pulled away.

"Hey," I said, "is that the only reason you kiss—for medicinal purposes?"

She shook her head.

"Well, what's wrong then?"

"I just don't, uh, feel that I wish to . . . be hurt, is all."

"Hurt? *I'm* the one who was hurt. Remember?"

"You know what I mean."

I put my arms around her again.

"Alice?"

No response. I counted to ten.

"Alice?"

No response. I counted to fifteen and hugged her to me, gradually increasing the pressure until the count of twenty-five, whereupon I locked my arms and pressed my cheek against her hair. At the count of thirty I kissed her forehead. At thirty-five I kissed the bridge of her nose. At forty I kissed the tip of her nose. At forty-three her chin came slowly up, and at forty-seven I kissed her open lips.

At one hundred sixty I dropped my right hand to her left buttock and let it die there. At one hundred and eighty I let it come to life. At one hundred ninety-five she disengaged her lips and whispered: "You'd better say something fast or I'm going to cry."

Oh Lord, I said to myself.

"I love you, Alice," I said to her.

"I love you, Oliver," she said and resumed the kiss.

At two hundred thirty-five I led her back into the house, across the living room, out the door, down the steps and into my car.

"Oh, a sports car," she said. "What is it, a Corvair?"

At nine hundred eighty-seven we were out of the Brentwood hills, heading east on Sunset Boulevard.

"Where are we going?" she said.

At one thousand three hundred and five we hit Laurel Canyon Boulevard and the foothills.

"Gosh, it's dark out," she said.

At two thousand one hundred and four I slowed down, bounced up over the curb, rolled to a stop, shut off the motor and swung out of the car.

"Oooo, it's creepy here," she said.

Two thousand one hundred and ten. I unlocked the front door.

"Is this where you live?"

Two thousand one hundred and twelve.

"Yes."

Two thousand one hundred and fourteen.

"I think you'd better take me home."

Two thousand one hundred and sixteen. I gave her a sincere-type embrace. I said: "I love you, Alice."

"I love you too, Oliver," she said.

Two thousand one hundred and twenty-four. We went inside and I poured us each a glass of scotch.

Two thousand one hundred and eighty-four. I put my

left arm around her waist and with my right undressed first her, then me.

Two thousand two hundred and sixty-five. I carried her, chest pressed to naked chest, up to the bed, dropped her in and followed.

"I love you, Oliver," she said, and slipped her arms around my neck.

"I love you, Alice," I said, and slipped into the fourth dimension.

# 10

Now if I haven't already mentioned it, I, Oliver (pronounced "Ah, lover") Bloom, am a very conscientious lover, and also a very good showman.

I have read all the guidebooks. I know that the only good orgasm is a mutual orgasm. And I know that a woman is a much better sex partner when she feels loved. So whenever I make love to a woman I take great pains to convince her that I love her exactly as much as she loves me, and the only time it doesn't work is when the woman is *also* a good performer, in which case I devote so much of my energies toward convincing her I love her as much as I suppose she loves me, and she in turn devotes so much of *her* energies to appear to equal *my* apparent love, that we exhaust ourselves before we get anwyhere.

With Alice it was not very difficult. Once I had resigned myself to the task of making her feel loved, she responded very nicely.

Now it was morning and as I, who had awakened first, coldly contemplated my slumbering lady of the evening before I realized I was in for another session of honest work. For Alice, by the dawn's early light, looked less than lovely. Mascara, eyebrow pencil, lipstick and pancake make-up had deserted her many hours before and now she lay blonde-lidded, puffy-eyed, pale and disheveled.

I, my distaste tempered with tenderness at her trusting vulnerability, leaned over and kissed her droopy little breasts. The sleepy arms of Alice, quite independent of Alice herself, found me and pressed my head against her chest.

"I love you, Alice," I donated.

"Mmmmm."

I kissed her many times, slowly, methodically, easing her out of slumber, easing her into the act of love, and when she was finally awake she found she had nearly reached the summit in her sleep. We got to the top about the same time, ran up a flag claiming the territory for the International Brotherhood of Lovers, and then started down again, she reveling in her love, I reveling in my performance.

When we were all the way down I gave her another wondrous gift: "I love you, Alice."

Then I stretched and sat up.

"Hey," I said, "we're beginning to smell like a fish market. C'mon. Let's take a bath."

I went into the bathroom and ran the water in the tub.

Then into the kitchen and fixed us both some instant coffee and brought it to the bed.

Alice was sitting up, the sheet wrapped tightly around her, under her armpits. When I approached the bed, she turned away from me.

"Hey," I said, setting the coffee down on the floor, "what's wrong?"

"You're naked and I'm very ugly."

I sat down on the covers and put my arms loosely about her shoulders.

"Let's take those points one at a time, buddy," I said. "First of all, on point number one you are dead right. I am as mother naked as the day I popped into this big bright world. So are *you*, under that silly sheet. So are we both and so have we been for the past six or eight hours. We made love, remember? I was inside of you, remember? And I loved you in there, so why can't I love you out here?"

"Get me a robe please, Oliver. And my comb."

"Point two. You are not ugly. You are *uncombed*. You

are *unpowdered*. You are *unmascaraed*. But you are by *no* stretch of the imagination ugly. As a matter of fact," I said, nuzzling her cheek, "you are a very lovely young woman and I should like nothing better than to invite all the neighbors in to show them just how lovely you are."

She giggled in spite of herself, her head still averted.

"There's a good girl," I said. "Now then, in just ten seconds I am going to whisk that sheet off your lovely young body, we are going to look quite earnestly at each other, and then we are going to jump right into a steaming tub and relax in pure animal comfort. Ready? One . . ."

"No, Oliver. I can't."

"Two . . ."

"Honestly. You go ahead without me."

"Three four five."

"You're counting for nothing."

"Six seven eight nine ten. Here I come, ready or not."

I reached for the top of the sheet and tugged with all my might. She hung on gamely and it appeared to be a standoff, except the sheet split down the middle and I sat down quite suddenly on the floor. After the first stunned second we erupted into helpless laughter.

Gradually we stopped laughing. I stood up, helped her out of bed, and held her out at arm's length until she finally dropped her hands and we each drank in the other's strong and weaker points. Then I guided her over to the closet door, on the back of which was a full-length mirror, and we saw how we looked together.

104

"I like my body when it is with your body," I said, borrowing from e.e. cummings.

We watched ourselves touch each other here and there and we watched ourselves embrace and wave good-by and move off to the waiting bathtub.

She got into the steaming water and at first feared that the tub was not going to be big enough to hold us both. But I stepped right in after her, quite confident, having done the trick before. We soaped ourselves and each other here and there with the slippery washcloth. And then I sat back and studied her while she washed her dark blonde hair.

She seemed so womanly and so absorbed in being a woman that I leaned over, kissed her moist shoulder and said without the slightest trace of altruism: "I love you, Alice."

"Mmmmmmhmmm," she replied.

It was not the answer I was hoping for.

What happened was that I had been somewhat hurt by someone I hadn't dreamed was capable of hurting me. I felt a bit betrayed. I felt a bit like a sucker. I felt I had to somehow regain control.

Alice got out of the tub, toweled herself dry, put on my robe and began to fix her hair. I, who would have preferred to continue watching the fascinating phenomenon of a woman being a woman, wrapped myself in a bath towel, went into the kitchen and busied myself with breakfast deals.

"Hey," I called to her with calculated merriment,

"how do you want your eggs—up, over, on end, or what?"

"Scrambled."

"Oh. How about the coffee—with cream, with sugar, or with, uh, alacrity?"

"Black."

"Oh. Hey, maybe you'd like me to make us some *Irish* Coffee?"

"Nope."

"Oh."

The nope threw me. If it had been a plain no, it might have meant her earlier lack of response was due to guilt or self-hate or simple post-copulatory remorse. But nope suggested she was pretty much her own mistress. Not mine.

Aaach. Silly to let a little thing like that upset me, spoil my fun. Probably had a perfectly logical explanation, one that had absolutely nothing to do with me. Maybe she was just feeling unbeautiful again. Yeah. I'd go in and kid her out of it.

I turned off the eggs and went back to the bathroom.

"Hey, how's the hair?"

"Fine."

"Know something? You've got the loveliest, silkiest blonde hair west of the Continental Divide."

I gave her an appreciative kiss on the back of the neck.

"Weren't you making eggs or something?" she said.

"Uh . . . yeah. Hey, Alice?"

106

"Yes?"

"Are you sort of feeling . . . unlovely again?"

"Nope."

(Nope. How the hell do you cope with nope?)

"Would you like me to, uh, tell you how gorgeous you are or anything?"

"Nope."

I stood behind her at the mirror, watching myself watch her watch me until, feeling entirely useless, I shrugged and went back to the kitchen to give a little moral support to the eggs.

As the frying pan began to sizzle again, I thought I might have figured it: a good actor has to convince himself before he can convince others. I had merely said "I love you" so many times that we'd both half-begun to believe it. But if she did believe it, I no longer had anything to convince her of. What a pity. Well. Maybe I could make her feel a little unloved so that I could have the fun of convincing her all over again. Yes.

Alice came in and sat down at the table.

I looked her over carefully for about a minute, then shrugged.

"Well, don't worry about it," I said at last.

"Don't worry about what?"

"About anything. About your hair or anything."

"My hair? Is there something wrong with my hair?"

"Oh no! No, not at all. No. Nothing. Looks very interesting that way. Very . . . unusual."

"*Unusual.* You think my hair looks unusual?"

"Oh. No, not actually. Why do you say that?"

"That's what you said. You said my hair looks very unusual."

"Oh, I *am* sorry. What I meant was, it looks very *refreshing*. Very nice for a change."

"For a *change*. You mean you didn't like the way I had it before."

"Oh *no*. I mean *yes*."

"Then you just don't like the way I have it now. Well this just happens to be the only thing a woman can do with her hair after she's washed it. If you don't like the way people look after their bath then just don't invite them into the tub with you."

She looked like she was on the verge of tears.

"Well in that case," I said, "I don't care what anyone says, I think it looks marvelous."

"Don't . . . *patronize* me for heaven's sake," she said, and that was enough to kick her over the brink. She burst into tears.

I sprang from the table and gathered her up in my arms.

"I'm sorry, baby," I whispered. "God, I'm sorry. I don't know how I could've made you think I was patronizing you, because to me you look good enough to eat, you really do."

I rocked her gently in my arms and kissed her tears as they ran down her cheeks.

"Do you forgive me?" I asked.

"I . . . I suppose so." Sniff. "Yes."

"Good."

I ran a hand through her damp hair and laid my un-shaven cheek against it.

"I love you, Alice," I whispered.

Sniff. Snort. Blowing of nose.

"I love you, Oliver," she said.

The benevolent despot was back in power.

# 11

Alice and I spent a lot of time together after that. Frequently I would bring her to my house on Friday evening and not drive her back home till early Monday morning. Frequently we would not wear clothes all weekend.

Once, to buy marshmallows (which we toasted over the gas stove on forks), we drove to Hughes Market wearing only trench coats, tennis shoes and sun glasses.

Three teen-aged girls, mistaking us for movie stars, asked for autographs. Alice signed hers Jean Harlow. I signed mine Francis X. Bushman. The kids, having heard of neither, walked away disgusted and filed the autographs between shelves of Quaker Oats.

For my demi-anniversary of service at *Hayday* and PKC&R, I received two raises and bought a portable television with remote control. Alice and I logged many hours together in bed, remotely controlling the volume and changing the channels. During the entertainment portions of the shows we would fool around and play love games, but when it was time for a commercial I insisted on total silence. Already a journeyman writer of soap commercials myself, I spent much time studying my competition, scrutinizing the faces of ladies reacting ecstatically to the feel of a new detergent in the dishpan, recognizing in most the same expression I'd often seen on Alice's face during orgasm. ("Coming soon: *Adultery in the Dishpan.* Are American Women Cuckolding Their Husbands With Their Liquid Detergents? What Is A Product For The Cleaning Of Dishes Doing With A Name Like *Thrill?* In a frank and penetrating exposé, former adman Oliver Bloom fearlessly explores these and other questions vital to an understanding of the causes of sexual incompatibility in marriage.")

Once, as an experiment, I picked up a bottle of Thrill, poured some into a dishpan of hot water at home, pulled down the kitchen shades and plunged my hands into the water up to my elbows. I got no sexual response.

Suspecting it worked only on women, I got Alice to try it too. She assured me that she was thrilled a lot more by me than by Thrill, but I was never completely convinced and every so often when I called for her at her apartment I would sneak a peek into her bathroom to see whether she might have been bathing with Thrill on the sly.

On an uncharacteristically chilly Sunday evening in October, having just returned from Alice's apartment, I heard a car drive up and die outside my house. In a moment there was a knock at the door. I, my arms full of firewood, yelled, "Hold it," dropped the wood on the hearth, arranged it around the gas log, opened the door and peered into the night. Two faces, one a good deal furrier than the other, peered back.

"I just hope you don't have hamburgers for supper," said the unfurry one. "For the last three days we've had nothing but hamburgers." Both figures pushed past me into the house and slammed the door.

"Bernice," I said, walking backwards.

"Also Albert. Mention him too or he gets lonely."

"Well, this *is* a surprise."

"Mention him too or he gets lonely."

"What?"

"The d-o-g," she whispered, pointing.

"Oh yeah. Hi, Al babe."

Albert leaped up, placed his paws on my shoulders and mopped my face with a slippery tongue. I gave him a reassuring pat and backed away, wiping my mouth.

"He loves you," Bernice explained. "For months he did nothing but ask for you. I hardly knew what to tell him."

"I see. Well, sit down, sit down. What can I get you?" I said, still backing away.

"Unless you stop walking backwards, the only thing you can get me is nervous."

I stopped sheepishly and sat down.

"Nice cozy little place you have here," said Bernice looking around the room. "Not enough room for a ping-pong table, but it ought to do very nicely for the time being."

"For the . . . time being?"

"Until we can find a bigger place, I mean."

"We?"

"Albert and I."

I got up quickly, took three Bufferins without water, chewed them up, swallowed them and sat down again.

"Let's take that again from the top," I said.

"Albert and I thought we would give you a chance to return a kindness. We thought we'd come and share your hospitality for a while. Why, what's the matter, pussycat? You don't look happy."

"You thought you'd . . . come and share my hospitality for a while, is that it?"

"Yes. I do hope it won't be too much of an imposition."

"Imposition? To have a full-grown horse and a half-grown woman share my one and a half room house? Im-

114

position? How could you possibly think that would be an imposition?"

"Wonderful. See, Albert, I told you he wouldn't mind."

"Wait a minute. Wait just one minute here. I seem to recall that you have a household of your own somewhere. In Santa Monica, if memory serves me correctly. What are you kids doing, running away from home?"

"Same peppy, fun-loving old Oliver. Yes, I suppose you could say we were running away from home. Fact is, we got thrown out."

"Thrown out? Harry threw you out?"

"Harry. Good old hubby Harry. Mr. Baby, it seems, has outgrown me. He's already filed for a divorce, I understand. Well, who gives a damn. It really wasn't much of a marriage anyway. Hey, what do I call myself now —Miss Baby? Mrs. Baby, Retired? What?"

"So Harry threw you out, eh? Good for Harry. I never thought the big guy had it in him."

"Oh, he had it in him all right. He's really changed a lot. You wouldn't recognize him at all. So look, how's about giving us a hand unloading the car?"

Bernice got up in a businesslike manner and started for the door.

"You know, if I didn't know you were serious, I'd swear I didn't know you were serious," I said. "But the fact remains that you and Albert couldn't *possibly* move in with me, even if I wanted you to."

"Even if you *wanted* us to? Is that what you said—

even if you *wanted* us to? That's the thanks I get for bringing you back from the brink of death? That's the thanks I get for nursing you day and night like you were my own child? For taking you in when your landlady threw you out into the street? For letting you sit at my table and eat my food? For letting you sleep in my bed and use my body? That's the thanks I get? I did all this so that tonight, when my dog and I are homeless and alone and have nobody else to turn to, you can sit there and tell me we couldn't possibly move in with you, *even if you wanted us to?*" Bernice looked up to the rafters for commiseration. "That's the thanks I get," she explained to them.

I, sawing an imaginary violin, couldn't help but marvel at her performance. Even though I knew she knew I knew it was a performance, I still felt pretty guilty.

Bernice, sensing she had softened up her audience with good theater, now switched to a sincere approach.

"Oliver," she said humbly, "I guess we both know that's not the whole truth, what I just said. I guess perhaps I've used you more than I've helped you. And I guess that if I were in your shoes, I myself would not be as generous and forgiving as I am now asking you to be. But what I said before is at least partly true: Harry really did throw us out. And we really *don't* have anyone else to turn to."

"Why don't you just get another apartment? Or live in a motel? Or go home to mother or something?"

"Well, that's the really awful part. You see, when I told my folks that Harry was starting divorce proceedings, they disowned me. Disinherited me, whatever you call it. They cut me off without a penny, Oll. I spent every bit of cash I had on motels and hamburgers in the last three days. I'm flat broke. I coasted the last ten yards to your house on an empty gas tank. I don't even have a quarter to buy a gallon of gas and get out of here."

How much was true? How much was good theater? Now that I thought about it, I did remember hearing a car die when she drove up.

"Bernice," I said, "I'd like to help you out, but I just don't see how I can. I mean, I've got my own life to lead now. I have certain commitments. For one thing, I have a lady friend who just wouldn't understand your moving in with me. I suppose I could lend you a little money, but as for—"

"Money is not what I'm asking you for. Money is the least of my problems. How long do you think I could go on living in motels and eating hamburgers?"

"Well, then find another apartment. I suppose I'd be able to dig you up enough for a deposit and I'm sure you'll be able to find a nice little place without very much trouble before—"

"What will I do for furniture?"

"Get a furnished place, then. Lots of people live in furnished apartments, for God's sake. *I* did."

Bernice looked down at the floor and sagged.

Oh God, I thought—first hysterics, then sincerity, now quiet tears—I won't make it, I really won't.

"Oliver," said Bernice so softly I could barely hear

**117**

her, "a woman needs more than a dog and a furnished apartment. Don't you believe I could truly need to belong to a man?"

"No," I said just as softly, "I don't."

Tears without sobs spilled out of her eyes and down her cheeks and off the end of her nose. Albert began to whine piteously.

I knew I couldn't hold out for more than sixty seconds at best. If this scene weren't finished in sixty seconds I would be dissolved in her tears.

"Look," I said, bounding out of the chair and opening my dresser drawer, "money."

I peeled five twenty dollar bills off a roll I kept under the undershorts and dropped them in her lap.

The clock was running out. Fifty seconds to go.

"This will be enough to take care of a deposit on a furnished place and a night or two in a motel," I said, now springing for my jacket. "If you need any more than that, just let me know."

I put on my jacket. The tears and the clock were both still running. Forty seconds to go.

"I'll see what I can dig up for you in the way of a filing job at the places I work."

I zipped my jacket. Thirty seconds left.

"Right now I'm going to drive down to the Standard Station on Sunset Boulevard and get you a couple gallons of gas to get you started."

I opened the door. Twenty seconds. I was going to make it after all. I could even afford a final gesture.

"Say, in the meantime why don't you have a bite to eat? There's some T-bones in the freezer. Give Albert one too."

With ten seconds still remaining on the clock, I waved, stepped outside and closed the door behind me. The instant I reached my car I heard the crash. I hesitated at the car. I worried what had happened. I knew that if I went back now to find out, all was lost. I opened the door of my Corvette. I stopped. I sighed. I slammed the car door and walked slowly back to the house and put the key in the lock and turned the doorknob and was only seventy percent surprised to see Bernice stretched out on the hardwood floor, her faithful dog grieving over her lifeless body.

# 12

I suppose the only saving consolation, the last lone out-post of rationalized self-respect in my allowing the success of Bernice's campaign to move in on me, was the fact that when she fell out of the chair in her simulated swoon, she hit her head on the window ledge and actually knocked herself unconscious.

Albert and I called a doctor, then put her to bed and tended her diligently all through the night. The doctor had assured us he could find no damage other than a large lump on her forehead, but the next day I phoned in sick at the offices and drove her down to the U.C.L.A. Medical Center for an X ray.

She still seemed a little groggy when we were through, so I drove her back and put her in bed, undressing her as I had the night before because she assured me she was too weak to do so herself. I must confess to slight extraclinical emotions about such activity, and would like to go on record here with my firm conviction that—Hippocratic oaths notwithstanding—there has got to be a lot more hanky-panky in the hospital than the healthy ever hear about. And I regard with particular suspicion those young white-coated Kildares who decide to take their residency in gynecology.

Come to think of it, how does a woman feel about having a man whom she hardly knows handle her private parts? ("No, doctor, I don't allow it on the first visit. All you gynecologists seem to be interested in just one thing.")

On the other hand, what a drag the conjugal bed must be for those fellows. ("Oh for God's sake, Clare, not tonight. Don't you think I get enough of that stuff at the office?")

At any rate—and a pretty slow rate at that—Bernice continued to convalesce in my house. It was scarcely humane to make a convalescent sleep on the floor, so naturally she got my bed and Albert and I used sleeping bags. I don't suppose you've ever seen a dog in a sleeping bag before, particularly a large German shepherd, but Albert became so entranced with mine that, fearing I might have to share one with him one night when I was too sleepy to resist, I went down to the Army surplus store and got him one for his very own.

By the third night, the ludicrous aspects of earning over twelve hundred dollars a month and having to bed down on the floor in a sleeping bag began to get to me. Bernice claimed she was still too fragile to be moved from my bed, and I traumatically feared to become re-involved with her body, so I got a piece of lumber six feet long and nailed it perpendicularly to the head-board, bisecting my king-size bed into two equal sleeping areas by means of a neo-colonial bundling board. I thus felt able to return to my bed in safety.

This seemed to work fairly well for a while, though Alice was puzzled to find me showing up at her apartment many more times during the week to make love and never offering to take her back to Laurel Canyon on weekends. I told her I felt our love needed a change of pace and a change of place.

As far as I was able to tell, nobody knew about my strange bedfellow and her furry friend except my analyst, and what he thought about the whole arrangement, Freud only knows. When I first broached the subject, lying on the couch, I did hear a strange sound from behind me where the Incredible Shrinking Man was seated, scribbling. I'm not certain what it was, but it sounded like an eyebrow that had not been raised in a long while finally creaking upward.

Stuff like that can scare the hell out of you if you're

an analyst. You raise an eyebrow here, another there, and before you know it you find yourself actually reacting to things and even having opinions and making value judgments.

"What do you think of her moving in with me, Doc?"

"I think we ought to examine your own feelings regarding the development of the situation."

"Well, my own feelings regarding the development of the situation are that, mainly, Bernice decided to move in on me and so she did."

"Uh, the meaning I had intended to convey was, you see, that we ought to examine the feelings which you, yourself, had with regard to the development of the situation or, if you will, the events or motivations which, on the part of Bernice, led to a wish or desire or inclination to, as you put it, move in on you, and then, you see, on the other hand, as it were, the events and/or motivations which, on your part, led to a wish or desire or inclination to permit her to remain in your, uh, house."

"Oh."

I have nothing but respect for a man who has spent twenty-seven years of his life (including kindergarten) in school, training for his profession. And it probably takes at least that long to learn how to keep your opinions to yourself. But I'm afraid that the restraints you must develop to accomplish this sort of thing are so inhibiting that they spoil you forever for a good simple declarative sentence. God forbid that my analyst's house should ever catch fire. ("Dear, the house, or, rather, the apartment, is, or, at least, in so far as I am able, at present, to ascertain, without, you see, committing ourselves to any rigid or irrevocable position, in the process, at least ostensibly, of being burned or consumed or, at any rate, overheated, by fire!")

So the doctor continued to remain inscrutable, and I continued to wonder whether Bernice's chaste presence on the other side of the bundling board every night was doing me any psychic damage.

By about the third week, she was up and around, cooking my meals and cleaning the house and at least going through the motions of apartment hunting. Presumably she read the ads in the *L.A. Times* every morning and then went out and inspected all the apartments she could manage to squeeze in between the hours of three and four in the afternoon, which I understood was the only time she had free. It was useless to ask what occupied the rest of her time. She would only roll her eyeballs rafterward and recite all the tasks she daily did for me in exchange for bed and board (or, in our case, boarded bed).

Bernice seemed to be encountering great difficulties in finding a suitable apartment. The ones she saw were either too large or too small, too expensive or too cheap, and of course she had a good thing going for her with Albert, because very few landlords are anxious to rent to horses.

If you want to know the truth, I began to mind her presence less and less as the weeks went by. She was a pretty good housekeeper and a hell of a cook, and since active sex was not a part of our relationship, it was sort of like being married. This, surprisingly, was not a to-tally disagreeable state.

I won't pretend that my stepped-up sexual schedule with Alice completely obviated all lustful ideas about Bernice. But I never showered or bathed with Bernice, I encouraged her always to change clothes in the bath-room, and by bedtime—what with my two jobs and Alice and the normal pressures of everyday living—I was generally so tired that I was out cold the moment my head hit the pillow (or, as frequently happened, the bundling board).

To alleviate Alice's suspicions, every so often I would dismantle the bundling board, have Bernice pack up all her junk and take Albert on a nice drive in the hills, while I brought Alice back to my house for a session of love or a bath or both. I can't truthfully say that Alice's suspicions disappeared entirely, but at least she couldn't feel that they were founded on fact. As an extra precaution, I made Bernice promise never to answer the telephone, which apparently she abided by, for I called a couple of times after leaving her in the house and it just kept ringing.

At the end of the sixth or seventh week a subtle change began to take place in Bernice. She began to be very solicitous about my general creature comforts. Was the soup hot enough? Were the martinis cold enough? Was the chair comfortable enough? Was there a draft on my back? Did I want her to knit me a sweater?

When I questioned her about these things, she replied that she was beginning to feel closer to me, in a sisterly way of course, and that whatever changes I might have noticed in her stemmed only from that. Consistent with her new sisterly attitude, she frequently came up and gave me a sisterly kiss on the forehead or a sisterly massage of the neck or a sisterly lick of the ear.

"Bernice, honey?"

"Yes?"

"What did you just do there?"

"I dunno. To your ear, you mean?"

"Yes, to my ear."

"I dunno. Guess I gave it a little lick with the old tongue-a-rooney there."

"Tell me. That, by you, is a sisterly deal?"

"A little lick on the ear with the old tongue-a-rooney?"

"Yeah."

"I dunno. Have you ever had a sister?"

"No."

"Neither have I. So how do we know—maybe that's a sisterly deal."

Other things began to happen. In her sleep Bernice began to toss and turn and often sprawl her arm across the bundling board. Sometimes her hand would only land on my chest. More often it would land on a more sensitive spot.

"Bernice?"

"Nnnh."

"Bernice, wake up!"

"Mmmff? Oh, whassamatter, Oll?"

"Your hand."

"My hand?"

"You're roamin' in the gloamin' again."

"Oh." Giggle. "Guess I am. Sorry."

"Yeah."

And still other things. Bernice became curiously absent-minded. She began to forget the simplest of details. She would sometimes forget to close the bathroom door when she changed clothes. She would sometimes forget to use the bathroom for that purpose altogether. She would sometimes forget which side of the bed was hers, and I would almost climb in on top of her in the dark if I came home after she'd turned off the lights. Once she even forgot I was taking a bath five minutes after I got into the tub:

"Bernice? Was there something you wanted in here?"

"Huh? Oh *hi*, Oll. Gosh, I forgot you said you were going to bathe now. I'm sorry."

"O.K."

"O.K."

"O.K.

"Oh, Oll, do you mind if I get an aspirin out of the medicine cabinet as long as I'm in here?"

"Go ahead."

"Thanks."

"Got it?"

"Yep."

"Good. Uh, was there anything else you wanted?"

"No, not really. Hey, Oll?"

"Yes?"

"Want me to scrub your back for you?"

"No thanks, that's not necessary."

"I don't mind, really I don't."

"Yeah, well, it's not necessary, thanks. I've got long arms."

"Mmmmm. Muscular too."

"Look, Bernice, if you don't mind, I'd prefer that you—"

"Oll?"

"What?"

"Please, just let me scrub your back for you. Like Alice does."

"How do you know what Alice does?"

"Doesn't she?"

"I hardly see that it's any concern of yours what Alice does or does not do for me."

"What's the matter? Are you embarrassed to have your old roomie see you in the nude?"

"No, I am not embarrassed to have my old roomie see me in the nude."

"Afraid?"

"Of what would I be afraid?"

"That you might lose control and . . . rape me?"

"I regret to say that losing control and raping you does not happen to be one of my major fears."

"I'll bet that's it. I'll bet you're afraid you'll lose control and just rape the living hell out of me."

129

"Nonsense. I have complete control."

"Oh, then you do admit that you have to employ some sort of control to prevent that from happening."

"I admit no such thing."

"You do admit, however, that the thought has crossed your mind."

"I admit nothing."

"Prove it."

"Prove what?"

"Prove that you have complete control. Prove that you can allow me to wash your back without attacking me."

"You're crazy."

"Afraid?"

"Not at all."

"Fine."

She sat down beside the tub, took the bar of soap and washcloth out of my hand and began to scrub my back.

Then:

"Hey, my back doesn't go that far down."

"Beginning to lose control, eh?"

"Of course not."

"Then be quiet."

Then:

"Hey, now that's not even anywhere *near* my back. That's not even in the same *hemisphere* as my back."

"Losing control?"

"NO, I'M . . . No, I'm . . . not."

Then:

130

"Hey, what're you doing? Bernice, you just had a bath this morning."

"I know, but I feel dirty again."

And before I could reply, she had flopped in the tub on top of me. I struggled halfheartedly for perhaps two minutes, then whispered "Sorry, Alice," grabbed Bernice by both shoulders and raped her. If that's what you want to call it.

"O.K.," I said, standing up, stepping out of the tub into the young lake we had created on the tiled floor, "you proved your point. I have no control. Absolutely no control. Are you happy now?"

"Very happy, pussycat," she said, stepping out of the tub and embracing me. "Alice has really gotten you in shape. You're really pretty good now."

"You don't say."

"Yes," she said, "I do," placing her head against my chest in a manner that I seemed to recall seeing somewhere before.

"Oll?"

"Yeah."

"I almost liked it that time."

"Swell."

"No, really. It was kind of fun."

"Swell."

"Do you think there's any hope for me, Oll?"

"How do you mean?"

131

"I mean do you think I'll ever be able to . . . to make it? Like other ladies?"

"I don't know, Bernice."

"Will you help me? Will you make love to me again, Oll?"

"Now? You mean right now?"

"No, I mean in general. Will you, Oll? Can we take that dumb bundling board off the bed? It's awful hard changing the sheets around that thing. Can we, Oll?"

"We'll . . . take the bundling board off the bed, if you like."

"And what about the other? Will you make love to me again? Will you, please, Oll? I want you so much. I really do. I've spent almost nine weeks seducing you."

"I know."

"But it wasn't just to seduce you. I wanted to prove to you how sorry I am for the way I treated you before. I wanted to show both of us that I can be nice to live with too. Harry's kicking me out really sort of shocked me out of something, you know? I think that when the first Baby started to grow up he kind of set an example for the second one too. I've been practicing being grown up ever since. Can I go on practicing with you, Oll? Can I stay here for a while longer and be your second lady? You can still go on seeing Alice. I don't care about her. O.K.? Is that O.K.? Can I stay and keep on practicing?"

"I . . . uh, guess so, Bernice. What would you like to do after you've grown up—go back to Harry or stay on with me or what?"

"Neither. I guess I'm still searching for the handsome

132

prince who will bring me True Love on a white charger. Maybe when I'm grown up I'll have a better idea of where to find him."

"Yeah, well you might just find . . . Aaah, never mind."

"What?"

"It's not important."

"I might just find *what?*"

"You might just find . . . a mop and dry up this floor before all the furniture floats away."

# 13

Maybe it was because Bernice and I were sort of back together again, or maybe it was only nice to think of it that way, but I found myself taking renewed interest in my work.

For one thing, since I was no longer physically frustrated at home, I could view the naked ladies at *Hayday* more objectively and was able to free myself for the sober task of making the magazine a serious art form.

I went to typography exhibits and returned, inspired, to the office to pore over type specimen books and to select only the most elegant fonts for the magazine. I went to photography exhibits and returned, inspired, with new shooting suggestions for our free-lance photographers. Under my tasteful tutelage, these erstwhile cheesecake servers dared to experiment with focus and lighting, color and composition. Stock poses, heavy make-up and pseudo-seductive leers gave way to spontaneous gestures, naturally colored cheeks and wistful smiles.

The change was apparent in the models themselves. Once they understood the look I was trying to give them, once they realized that they increased rather than decreased their femininity by making their appeal softer and subtler, a remarkable metamorphosis began to take place. Before my very eyes, tough-talking strippers and B-girls became demure coeds in pageboy hairdos and gingham frocks. A few even took to blushing when they disrobed in the studio.

The photographic results were spectacular. But in my idealism I had inadvertently sown the seeds of my own undoing.

My first hint of what lay ahead came at the end of a particularly brilliant shooting session with a part-time call girl by the name of Avis Hertz. The last three or four weeks had seen Avis shed not only superfluous bodily attire but superfluous facial attire as well, emerging as a woman of such stunning natural beauty that only her somewhat nasal voice survived as evidence that it was still the same person inside.

"Mr. Bloom," said Avis, zipping herself into a frilly, high-necked dress that I hadn't seen before, "I hafta tellya something important."

"Yes, Avis?"

"I don't know howta say this exackly, Mr. Bloom—on account of you're really the one that was responsible for all the nice things that's been happening to me lately?"

"Yes?"

"Well, y'see, it's my fella. Arthur? I mean I met him about two weeks ago. On my night job, y'know? When I came over to his house the first time, he didn't believe I was the girl he had called. I mean I guess I looked so wholesome and everything—on account of the way I've been dressing and making up since I've been modeling here? So anyway, we got into this big discussion about men and women and life and stuff, and we kinda talked the night away without ever getting down to business, and he said he wanted to be my fella and I should give up all my other clients and everything, and I did and we've been going out together ever since. Arthur said last night he wants to marry me."

"Why, Avis, that's marvelous. Congratulations!"

"Thanks. So I'm afraid I'm gonna hafta give up the modeling too. Arthur says it's not dignified."

I thought at first that she was kidding, that she was parodying the plot of a current musical comedy. But she wasn't. She was dead serious. I didn't know what to

137

say to her. I had taken a call girl who didn't even get enough calls to make her a full-time girl and transformed her into somebody's fiancée and all the thanks I was getting was the implication that I was no longer dignified enough to be her employer. I was beginning to feel a little hyperacidity in the lower digestive track but I am, I suppose, essentially a romantic, so instead of trying to bind her to me with ties of guilt, I managed a wishy-washy smile and washy-wished her the best of luck.

The next day another of my models—a stripper who did special material with cabbage leaves and a trained rabbit—decided she'd had enough of salad days and modeling and, thanking me from the bottom of her bottom, put on her clothes and went back home to finish college.

The third day the third lady withdrew. The fourth day the fourth. And by the end of the week I was fresh out of flesh. I took my problem to Landsdown.

"Sounds to me like they were baring their souls when they should have been baring something else, Bloom," he said.

"Yeah, well, I had no idea it would turn out this way, y'see."

"A smart art director wouldn't have let that happen, Bloom. What do you think I'm paying you to do here, save souls?"

"No."

"No, *sir*."

"No, *sir*."

"You think I'm paying you to help fallen women hold their heads a little higher, Bloom?"

"No, sir."

"Sounds to me like you're spending too much time on social work and not enough time on art work."

"ALL I WAS . . . All I was trying to do was put a little class into the magazine, sir. I didn't realize it would backfire like that."

"Well, it *did* backfire. And where are you keeping all these classy photographs anyway—you got any around?"

"Here, you mean?"

"Here."

"Well, yeah. I guess there's a few in my office, but they're not cropped or color-corrected or anything like—"

"Let me see them."

"Well, they're not really ready to—"

"Let me see them."

"But they're not in any shape to—"

"*Let me see them.*"

"All *right*, all *right*."

I went to my office and brought back the best transparencies.

"Here."

Landsdown took the first one and held it up to the light.

"What's wrong here?"

"What's, uh, wrong where?"

"Here. With this shot. It's all out of focus. That's wrong. Why did you do it wrong, Bloom?"

"Out of focus? Oh, that's not out of focus, that's a diffused effect."

He raised his chin and held the photograph out at arm's length.

"Looks to me like it's out of focus. Let me see another one."

I handed him another one. He took it, looked at it and then at me.

"This one's overexposed," he said.

"Oh no," I smiled, "That's called high-key lighting. It's very chic."

He took a third photo out of my hands.

"And this one here is *under*exposed."

"No," I said, "that one's—"

"—low-key lighting, I suppose. Swell. But it still looks underexposed. What have you been doing to our photographers, Bloom—helping them hold their heads a little higher? Let them keep their heads where they are, Bloom, so they can see into the camera."

He regarded me thoughtfully. "You know," he said, "I don't understand it. These people used to take very good pictures—clear, sharp, well-lit pictures. They shot a photograph of a naked woman and you could damn well tell it was a naked woman. Look at these. Every one is either so blurred or so washed out or so poorly lit that you can't tell whether it's a picture of a naked woman or a goddam rain cloud."

"I was only trying to upgrade the book a little," I said. "I was only trying to give it a little class. You've got to move with the times, Landsdown. How long do you think you can go on being the Vulgar Picture King?"

Landsdown did not hit me. He hit the intercom button. With his fist.

"Miss Selfridge!"

"Yes, sir?"

"Come in here and take a memo! On the double!"

Miss Selfridge was off the intercom and into the office while the word "double" still hung in the air.

Landsdown leaned forward and began to dictate, snapping his jaws like a man-eating piranha fish.

" 'To: All *Hayday* photographers. Subject: Classy photography. You are hereby advised that all classy photography for this magazine will cease immediately. There will be no more fuzzy images. There will be no more underexposures. There will be no more overexposures. There will be breasts. There will be thighs. There will be backsides. And they will all be as clear and as obvious and as *vulgar* as you can possibly make them.' Miss Selfridge, type up a stencil, run it off on the mimeo, and have those memorandums in the mail in twenty minutes flat. Now stand tall and move out sharply. Dismissed!"

Miss Selfridge was off like a dirty shirt.

Landsdown turned to me.

"Now then, do you want to resign or shall I fire you?"

"Neither."

"What?"

"I'm staying."

"What do you mean you're staying?"

"Just exactly that. I'm staying. I'm not leaving. I haven't done anything wrong. I haven't done a thing except try to improve the magazine, so I am not resigning and I am not going to be fired."

"You . . . mean you really want to stay?"

"No, but I'll damn well not give you the satisfaction of kicking me out. I'll leave when I'm goddam ready to leave and not a goddam minute before!"

He stared at me for maybe fifteen seconds, then threw up his hands and burst out laughing. Very distinct ha-ha's all over the place, and not the slightest trace of a smile. Finally he calmed down, wheezed mopped his forehead, and stuck out a meaty hand.

"All right, Bloom, I like your spirit. You're full of the old piss and vinegar. Wish I had fifty more like you, by God. All right. Stay as long as you like. Just promise me you'll go back to vulgar pictures. Shake."

"I'm not shaking and I'm not promising either," I said and stalked out of the room.

"By *God*, I like your spirit," he called after me. "Hey, stop by the bookkeeper's desk and tell her I said to give you a fifty-buck raise."

"Tell her yourself, you bastard," I called back.

"BLOOM!"

His shout caught me in the small of my back. I turned around.

142

"Yes? Yes, sir?"

"Don't tickle the tiger's tail, Bloom. Piss and vinegar is one thing, but enough is too much. You understand? You hear me, Bloom?"

"Yes, sir, I hear you."

"Good. Now get the hell out of here and go do some work."

"Yes, sir."

We had, at least, communicated.

The minute I got back to my desk, Landsdown communicated again. This time it was by phone.

"Bloom?"

"Yes, sir."

"You were dead wrong on nearly everything you said in here just now, but there may be one small area where your hunch was correct."

"No. Honest?"

"All right, cut the sarcasm. I'm talking about your idea of using wholesome-looking girls in our pictures. There's something low and sneaky about that concept I think I like. You're pretty good at helping fallen women hold their heads higher, Bloom—you think you could help a few wholesome women hold their heads *lower?*"

"Sir?"

"I say do you think you could get us some wholesome-looking models?"

"Well, I don't know. I suppose so, sir."

"Swell. Look, why don't you start by running an ad in the *Times?*"

"An ad? In the *Times?*"

"Write it very innocent, but try to be a little smutty, too. You know what I mean?"

"I'm not sure," I said.

"Well, just slap out a rough draft and we'll go over it together, all right?"

"All right."

"Swell."

I hung up the phone and began scribbling words on my layout pad with a grease pencil:

*NICE YOUNG LADIES, aged 18-22, Our company is really awfully interested in hiring several bright, attractive young ladies of good moral character to assist us in the task of*

Too innocent. I tore it up and started again:

*WOMEN, 18-22. We are looking for several high-type females who are not so stuck up or prudish that they would mind doing a few things and making some easy money. We don't*

Too smutty. I tore it up and started again. After a while I wrote:

*MODELS WANTED. Apply Hayday Magazine.*

144

That had a certain straightforward quality I liked. I took it in to Landsdown and laid it on his desk.

"What's this?" he said.

"Your classified ad."

He read what I had written.

"That's . . . all you want to say in it?"

"Well, it's only a rough draft. Didn't you say just slap out a rough draft and we'll go over it together?"

"Uh, yes. But couldn't you take it any farther than this?"

"Well, I suppose I could have. But seeing as how I was so far off base on all that other stuff, I figured I'd come to you before I spent too much time on it."

"I see. Well, let's have a look."

Landsdown moved the line I had written so that it was directly between his elbows on the desk, adjusting his chin in his hands like the lens housing of some huge microscope till he had the words in proper focus. He continued to focus for perhaps five minutes, then, with one hand still supporting his chin, he reached for a soft pencil and began to scribble.

When he had lined out four or five scribbles, he crumpled the whole sheet of layout paper into a ball and, without even glancing at his target, hooked the ball over his left shoulder toward the wastebasket. It missed by a yard or more.

"You know what we need, Bloom?"

"What do we need, sir?"

"We need a professional ad writer."

"We do?"

145

"Yep."

Landsdown punched the intercom button.

"Miss Selfridge."

"Yes sir?"

"What's the name of that advertising outfit upstairs?"

"Plapert, Carstairs . . . Just a moment, sir. It's . . . Plapert, Kernig, Carston and Robbins, sir."

"Good. Get them on the phone."

"Surely."

"What do you, uh, want with *that* bunch?" I said.

"We need a professional ad writer, don't we?" he said.

"Mr. Landsdown, whom did you wish to speak with there?" said Miss Selfridge.

"The first one—Plapper?"

"Plapert. Very well, sir, I'll get him on the line."

"Listen," I said quite earnestly, "are you sure you want to bother them with a thing like this?"

"Of course I'm sure. What do you mean, *bother* them? We need an ad written. They write ads. How do you figure we're bothering them?"

"Well," I said, "the way they operate is they take a fifteen percent commission on all media charges. With our classified ad here, that comes out to about a dollar twenty."

"Mr. Landsdown," said Miss Selfridge, "I have them on the line—"

"Hang the expense," he said to me. "I'll take the call," he said to Miss Selfridge.

"—but Mr. Plapert is not in at present, sir," she said. "Is there someone else who can help you?"

146

"Oh. The second one, then—what's his name?"

"Kernig?" she said.

"Kernig. Get Kernig."

"Thank you, sir."

"What I meant was," I said, "they may not want to touch a job like that for only a dollar twenty."

"Well then, I'll offer them *five* bucks. *Ten* bucks. Whatever they like. I don't mind spending a little money to get the job done right."

"Mr. Landsdown," said Miss Selfridge, "Mr. Kernig is not in at present. Is there someone else who can help you?"

"What? Oh. Yes, the third fellow—what's his name?"

"Carston," she said.

"Carston. Get Carston."

"Thank you, sir."

"Are we even sure we want to get tied up with advertising people, sir?" I said.

"What do you mean?"

"Well, uh . . . you know what they say about advertising people, don't you, sir?"

"Oh yes. I see what you mean. Well, blast it, Bloom—we're not getting tied *up* with them, we're only—"

"Mr. Landsdown?" said Miss Selfridge.

"—asking them to do one lousy ad. I don't—"

"Mr. Landsdown?"

"—see how they could do us any moral damage just by preparing one lousy—"

"Mr. Landsdown?"

"—ad. Yes, Miss Selfridge, what *is it!*"

147

"Mr. Carston is not in at present either, sir. Is there someone else there who can help you?"

"*No*, Miss Selfridge, I'm afraid there isn't."

"Would you like to speak with Mr. Robbins, sir?"

"*No*, Miss Selfridge!" I yelled.

"Who?" said Landsdown.

"Mr. Robbins," she said. "He's the fourth partner."

"Is he in?" said Landsdown.

"Robbins?" I said. "Oh, you don't want to talk to *Robbins*."

"Shut up, Bloom, I can't hear. Is he in, Miss Selfridge?"

"Yes, sir," she said.

"Believe me, you don't want to get mixed up with Robbins, sir," I said.

"Shut *up*, Bloom. Yes, put him on, Miss Selfridge."

"Thank you, sir. You can pick up the phone now."

Landsdown picked up the phone.

"Robbins? Oh, well put him *on*, God damn you. . . . Thank you. Hello, Robbins? Fred Landsdown, *Hayday Magazine*. Say, what the hell's the matter—are you operating on a skeleton crew up there or what? . . . All right, never mind. Robbins, we've got an advertising problem we'd like you to help us out on. . . . Right. . . . Well, no, I don't think we need a conference. I can tell it to you right over the phone. We . . . Well, I don't think we *need* a conference. . . . No. No, it's not that compli— Look, can I just tell you what the problem is? Then, if you still think we need a conference, I'm willing to . . . Fine. All right, what we've got here is a *Times* classified ad. We're trying to . . . What? A *Times* classified ad. . . . Yes. . . . No, that was really all we . . . I see. Well, that's very kind of you. Thanks. Thanks very much. I'll send it right up. So long."

Landsdown hung up the phone with a puzzled frown.

"What'd he say?" I said.

"Said to send it right up and they'd do it free of charge. Said he'd take care of it personally. Pretty decent of the man, I'd say."

"Ah, well, just the sort of sneaky trick you'd expect from that bunch."

"How do you mean?"

"They're playing with you, sir. By doing this job free, they're placing you in their debt. And for what—for a lousy dollar twenty. Don't go through with it, sir. It's only a dollar twenty *this* time, sure. But next time it'll be higher—maybe two dollars, maybe even five. And the next time it'll be even higher. Ten. Then twenty. Then thirty. Who knows how far they'll decide to push it. These men are ruthless sir, they'll stop at nothing. You could end up with thousands of dollars of free work from these people—a debt you could never hope to repay. Stop now, sir, I beg you. Stop now, before it's too late."

Landsdown swung around in his chair, rolled a sheet of yellow paper into his typewriter and tapped out a few lines with his first two fingers. Then he pulled the sheet out and handed it to me.

"That's all they need to know," he said. "If they have any further questions, I think you can answer them."

"What?"

"Don't just stand there, Bloom—get moving."

"Moving, sir?"

"Upstairs, upstairs. Seventh floor, I think."

"You want *me* to take it up there?"

"Why not? You're the one that started this whole thing, aren't you? You're the one who objected to our vulgar models, aren't you? Well, here's your chance to get a few you like. What are you waiting for, Bloom?"

"I don't know."

"Is there some reason why you can't take care of this matter right now?"

"Oh, well, uh, no, not actually, sir."

*"Then get the hell out of here."*

"Uh, well all right."

I somnambulated out of his office, down the hall, out into the reception room, into the elevator, and up to seven.

"Hi, Mr. Bloom," said the PKC&R receptionist, as I drifted past her, along the hall and up to Robbins' office.

"Hi, Oliver," said Robbins' secretary. "You want to see Mr. Robbins?"

I nodded dreamily.

"Go right in," she said.

I drifted in.

Robbins was sucking his pipe and studying Hollywood Boulevard as I entered. He wasn't aware of my presence, and I hadn't absolutely decided to enlighten him.

"Mr. Bloom is here, sir," said his secretary.

"Bloom? Oh, hello, Bloom. Sit down, boy."

He swiveled around to face me.

I sat.

"What you got there—something for me?" he said.

When I didn't reply, he reached across the desk and took the paper out of my hand.

"Where'd you get this, Bloom?" he said.

"Get what, sir?"

"This paper. What you had in your hand just now."

"Oh, that. I got that from . . . Mr. Landsdown."

"Landsdown? What were you doing down there?"

"Down there? Oh, how do you figure I was down there?"

"Well then, how did you get this?"

"A . . . messenger brought it up. A messenger brought it up and I just brought it right in to you."

"Oh. I thought you said you got it from Landsdown."

"Well, I did. I mean, in the sense that he was the point of origin, I got it from him. Or, more properly, *you* got it from him, the messenger and/or I serving only in the capacity of middlemen."

"I see," he said, not seeing. He looked it over and nursed his pipe. "Do you know anything about this?"

"Well, not . . . as much as I'd like to," I said.

"This fellow Landsdown. Calls me a few moments ago. Says he's got an advertising problem he wants us to help him out on. Fine, we'll call a conference and talk it over, I tell him. No, he says, I'll just tell it to you over the phone. Over the phone, right? Are you ready for that? Well, it's just as easy to arrange a small confer-

151

ence, I say—I'll bring a few of my boys down and we can kind of kick it around together. No, he says, no conference. I'll just tell it to you over the phone. Are you ready for him? Look, I say, give me some idea of what the problem is and if you still prefer to do it over the phone, I can bring a few of my boys in on the line and we can kick it around together over the phone. O.K., he says. Well, you'll never guess what he wanted. Go on, guess."

"A classified ad?"

"How did you know that?" he said, robbed of his punch line.

"I read what it said on the paper there. It says 'Classified Ad.'"

"Oh. Well. Anyway, I almost burst out laughing. You know what we'd net on a job like that?"

"About a dollar twenty."

"Yeah. And I understand this fellow is really loaded, too. Big house in Brentwood. An orgy every weekend. Always wondered what goes on at that magazine. So I told him I'd do the ad for him free of charge. Maybe we'll get invited to an orgy, eh? Want to tackle it?"

"Tackle what?"

"The ad."

"Not particularly."

"Go ahead, do you good. You can even deliver it in person if you like."

"Goody."

"There's a boy. If you have any questions, give Landsdown a ring."

"Listen, Robbins," I said, "can I speak freely?"

"You kidding me? Of course. What is it, Bloom?"

"Well, I don't know quite how to say this, but . . . are you sure you want to get us tied up with a sex magazine?"

"How do you mean, tied up?"

"Well, if we do an ad for them, that makes them our client, doesn't it? How do you suppose our other clients are going to feel about our being tied up with a sex magazine?"

"Yezmhmm. Well, I see your point there, Bloom." Pause. "Aah, look. We're not really taking them on as a client at all, not if we don't accept any money from them. Look. This doesn't have to involve the agency at all. It's just a favor you and I are doing for Landsdown, O.K.? It's just between you and me and Landsdown, and nobody else ever has to know anything about it. O.K.? What do you say, kid?"

"Well, all right. Just so long as we keep it quiet. I wouldn't want the agency's name dragged through the mud."

"You kidding me? Mum's the word, Bloom."

He winked.

I winked back.

He gave me a little squeeze on the arm.

I settled for another wink and left.

In my upstairs office, I filled the wastebasket with crumpled balls of paper before I finally settled on the exact wording. I took it in to Robbins, who looked at it

153

briefly, nodded and patted me on the shoulder. Then I took it downstairs to Landsdown.

"Certainly took your time up there," he said. "Well, let's have a look."

He cleared his throat and read aloud:

> NICE YOUNG LADIES, aged 18-22. Our company is really awfully interested in hiring several bright, attractive young ladies of good moral character to assist us in the task of upgrading an already widely accepted product. Part time. Excellent pay. Pleasant surroundings. Reply Box 8322."

"What do you think, sir?" I said.

"Not bad. A bit heavy-handed in the sincerity department, but not bad. Quite a difference when it's handled by a professional, wouldn't you say?"

"My very thought. All the difference in the world, sir."

"Good. Good. Tell them to run it in this Sunday's *Times*. Oh, and, Bloom—"

"Yes sir?"

"Insist on paying for the space."

"I'll do that, sir," I said.

The following Sunday I picked up Alice's *Times* and checked the classified section to see if our ad had run as scheduled.

154

"What are you looking for, Oliver?" said Alice from behind her Peanuts.

"Oh, just some dumb ad we're running at *Hayday* to get new models."

"Say! You'll never guess who called me the other day."

"Bertrand Russell."

"No. Fred Landsdown."

"Fred Landsdown? How do you know Fred Landsdown?"

"Think. Where did you first meet me?"

"Oh? Oh! Well, son of a gun. How do you like that. What did he want—invite you to another party?"

"No. He wanted to know if I'd model for *Hayday*."

"He did? Why, that old lecher. What'd you tell him?"

"Well, I thought he was joking at first. He said I was exactly the type you were looking for."

"He did? That's absurd. What'd you tell him?"

"Why is it absurd?"

"Why? Well, I don't know, it just is. Don't *you* think it's absurd?"

"What type *are* you looking for?"

"What type? I don't know. But I just don't see you in *Hayday Magazine*."

"Why not? Isn't my body good enough?"

"I don't know. Sure, it's good enough. That's not the point. You told him no, didn't you?"

"What *is* the point?"

"The point is that, uh . . . that you aren't the type, that's all."

155

"Fred said you're looking for very wholesome, innocent-looking girls. Don't you think I'm wholesome and innocent-looking any more?"

"Oh, well, yes, sure I do. You told him you would, is that it?"

"I told him I wouldn't, but now I'm beginning to wonder if I did the right thing."

"Oh, Alice. Do you seriously expect me to believe you wouldn't be embarrassed to take off your clothes in front of all those people?"

"All what people?"

"The photographer. His assistants. The other girls. Whoever happened to be in the studio at the time. And what about our readers? You really want to display your bare hide to all our readers?"

"Maybe I don't and maybe I do."

"This is the girl that was embarrassed to let a man who had made *love* to her look at her body the morning after, right?"

"That was different. That was a long time ago. Besides, I've changed a lot since then."

"Boy, you can say that again."

"Seems to me you're the only one who'd be embarrassed if I *did* model."

"Me. Me? *I'd* be embarrassed? Why would *I* be embarrassed? Listen. If you want to go running around town showing off your bare boobies to total strangers, you just go right ahead and do it, all right? I couldn't care less. They're your boobies, not mine. So you just go

156

right ahead and do whatever you like with them. All right?"

"All right. Maybe I just *will* run around and show them off to total strangers."

"Good."

"Maybe it's not such a bad idea after all."

"Fine."

"Maybe I'll just go right ahead and do that."

"Swell. Marvelous. I sincerely hope you do."

# 14

Monday I was tied up nearly all morning in a client conference at the agency. Our soap man had come over for a screening of his latest commercial and, upon seeing it, was immediately overcome by the congenital client aberration of *jamais vu*.

Just as someone who is experiencing *déjà vu* suddenly imagines that a conversation in which he is currently engaged has all occurred before in every detail, so someone experiencing *jamais vu* suddenly imagines that a commercial which he has approved before in every detail is totally unfamiliar to him.

As soon as our client began to display the telltale symptoms and bring up suggestions for revisions, we (the account executive, the art director, the traffic man, Robbins and I) immediately sent for the agency's resident mirror man. Like the distorting mirrors in carnival fun houses, the agency mirror man deftly reflects all the client's ideas in such a distorting manner that the client sees how absurd they are and withdraws them in embarrassment. When the client has been drained of all his own bad ideas by a good mirror man, he is then too weak to resist someone else's.

Needless to say, a mirror man must be awfully fast at anticipating replies. Ours, who was known to this particular client as Steve, was so quick he could mirror even the most casual of remarks.

"Oh, look, sir," said the account man, distracting the client's attention to our newest arrival, "here comes Steve."

"Hello, Steve," said the soap man. "Good seeing you again."

"Been quite a while since you've seen me, eh, sir?" said the mirror man.

"Yes, that's . . . No, come to think of it, I believe I saw you as recently as last week."

"Steve," said Robbins, "we were just going over some thoughts on our new washday product, Improved Throb in the pink plastic squeeze bottle."

"Yes, Steve," I added, "Mr. Scantlebury has just raised a few suggestions for revisions on the commercial which we feel are certainly worth noting."

"Why don't you repeat some of your ideas, sir, to kind of bring Steve up to date on this thing?" said the account exec.

"Well," said the soap man, "all I said was, it seems to me that we can come up with something a little more inventive for the first scene than a housewife standing in the kitchen with her hands in the dishpan, wondering why her husband is no longer attentive to her."

"Tell him your idea, sir," said the account man.

"I think I'd prefer that Mr. Scantlebury tell me his idea himself in his own way," said the mirror man with an encouraging wink toward the client.

"Well," said the soap man, "my thought was to have a sort of impromptu interview, you see, between—"

"Excuse me," said the mirror man, "but my own feeling for a long time, as you know, has been that we should adopt the approach that people like Rambler, Tide, Gleem, Personna and Excedrin have used so successfully in the past—the one where a hidden camera is set up in a studio and people are asked their impromptu reactions to a particular product. While it's not, I must confess, the freshest approach in the world, and while there are certain inherent production drawbacks, like, for example, the enormous amount of footage that must be shot before any sort of favorable reactions can be captured on film—reactions, of course, free from profanity or any reference to a competing brand—still, I

161

feel that it is a very sound approach and one that we ought to explore. Forgive me for interrupting you, Mr. Scantlebury, but I'd really like to get your reaction to that before you tell me your own idea."

"Ah, well, Steve," said the soap man, "I think it's a fine idea, but, as you point out yourself, it's, uh, scarcely the freshest approach in the world."

In this manner, the housewife whose husband was no longer attentive to her with her hands in the dishpan was reinstated and the commercial was eventually saved.

When the conference broke up, I raced downstairs to *Hayday*.

"Sorry I couldn't get here sooner," I said, trotting briskly into Landsdown's office, "but you've got to watch those typographers like a hawk, boy. Say, how'd we do on the ad for models?"

"We're all set," said Landsdown.

"Swell. Let me have all the replies—I've got a harem scene to cast."

"I told you we're all set," said Landsdown.

"What do you mean?"

"I mean that, since you weren't here to do your job, I did it for you. I called half a dozen of the lovely ladies in here this morning, chatted a while, looked over their . . . qualifications, and cast your harem scene. Shooting is tomorrow at ten."

"You're putting me on, of course."

"Not in the least. Somebody has to do the work

around here, Bloom. You weren't around to do it, so I simply did it for you."

"I see. So now you're not only telling my photographers how to shoot, you're also selecting my models for me."

"*My* photographers, Bloom. *My* models."

"I don't know whether you realize it, sir, but you are gradually taking over the duties of the art director. You are gradually dispensing with the need for my services."

"A good man, Bloom, makes himself indispensable to the organization by virtue of his demonstrable skill and efficiency. If I am indeed able to dispense with your services, then maybe I should."

I said nothing in reply.

"I'll be at the shooting tomorrow," he said, "to see just what it is you contribute in that particular area."

"Fine," I said. "I'll look forward to seeing you there."


By the time I reached the studio Tuesday morning, Landsdown and a couple of the models had already arrived. I was not overly surprised to see that Alice was one of those present, but I *was* somewhat baffled to see Avis Hertz.

"Avis," I said, "I thought you felt modeling for *Hayday* wasn't dignified."

"I'll tellya something very frankly, Mr. Bloom," she said, motioning me away from the others. "I didn't know it was *Hayday* when I answered the ad. In the

Sunday *Times?* But when I went over for the interview, I immediately recognized the building."

"So how come you agreed to do it?"

"Very frankly, Mr. Bloom, I wasn't gonna. But that gentleman over there—Mr. Landsdrown . . .?"

"Landsdown. Yes?"

"He was so pleasant when I came over, we got into this big discussion about men and women and life and stuff, and I kinda developed a whole *thing* for him. A crush, y'know?"

"What about Arthur?" I said. "I thought you were going to marry Arthur."

"That creep? You kidding me? He was just trying to get around paying my fee. Are you ready for guys like that? Say," she said in a more confidential tone, "ya don't think old Landsdrown's trying to pull the same kinda stunt, doya?"

"I wouldn't know, Avis," I said. "He does seem about to launch some sort of economy drive. But right now I think you'd better go and get dressed. Or undressed, as the case may be."

"Right, Mr. Bloom. Talk to ya later."

She scurried off to the dressing room.

"So, Alice," I said, striding up to her, "I see you decided to show the world your boobies after all."

"Fred said from what he could tell they'd work out fine."

"Oh, Fred said that, did he? Well, I'm sure you won't lack for admirers once these pictures appear. Incidentally, were you planning to take off your clothes for this

164

shooting, or were you hoping the photographer could somehow fake it?"

"Don't worry," she said, "nobody here will have to fake anything." She picked up a length of pink gauze which was lying on the prop table. "Are these the little costumes we're supposed to be wearing?"

"That's right."

"Splendid," she said, and ambled away from me with what she imagined to be a lascivious motion.

"Hey, Landsdown," I said, "that's only two. Where's our third girl?"

"She'll be here," he said, "don't worry."

With everybody telling me not to worry, I was beginning to feel very relaxed. I continued to feel relaxed for about fifty-two seconds, whereupon a friendly bark and two familiar faces unlaxed me quite thoroughly.

"Hi, everybody," said Bernice. "Stand by to roll 'em!"

"Wurff!" said Albert, joyfully knocking over a light stand.

"Stop that, Al. Sorry I'm late, folks. I'll be in the raw in two shakes."

"That's the third one," said Landsdown. "Miss Baby, come over here and meet our art director."

Bernice bounced over.

"Miss Baby, Mr. Bloom," said Landsdown.

"Charmed, Mr. Bloom. You can call me Miss Baby. Hey, does everybody know Albert?"

There were scattered lukewarm greetings for Albert.

"Hey, you'll have to do better than that," she said in a hoarse stage whisper, "he's very s-e-n-s-i-t-i-v-e."

165

There were heartier greetings for Albert, which he acknowledged by scrubbing a few faces with his tongue.

I picked up a length of gauze.

"Oh, Miss Baby, may I have a word with you?" I said, grabbing Bernice by the arm and yanking her out of earshot. "Now then," I whispered, "have you gone out of your mind or what?"

"Why, what's the matter, pussycat? I'm just trying to hustle a little cash to keep the home fires burning. I thought you'd be pleased."

"Pleased!"

"Yes, I saw the ad in the *Times* and it said part-time work and good pay, so I answered it. I was going to surprise you. I didn't know it was for *Hayday*."

"You did find out eventually, I presume?"

"Yep. But I couldn't see any harm in it. Besides, I think it'll be fun."

"Fun? Making a public spectacle of yourself you think is fun?"

"Oh, simmer down, Oll. What's so terrible about taking pictures in my birthday suit? I did it all the time when I was little."

"Yes, but you're not little any more. At least not physically. Did you tell Landsdown anything about us? Or about the agency?"

"Of course not, silly. Why would I do a thing like that?"

"O.K., just see that you don't. Now there's one other

thing. By some strange coincidence, one of the models—"

"Bloom," Landsdown called, "please pursue women on your own time."

"Boy, what a grouch *he* is," said Bernice.

"You're telling me. Now look, you remember Alice—"

"Alice? Alice who?"

"Mr. Bloom?"

"Oh. Yes, Avis?"

"I'm all ready, Mr. Bloom."

"Yes, I can see you are, Avis. Good. Now if you'll just—"

"Mr. Bloom?"

"Yes, Avis?"

"That other girl. With the glasses? Alice?"

"Yes," I said, "what about her?"

"Alice?" said Bernice. "That Alice is here? *Your* Alice is modeling?"

"*Your* Alice," said Avis. "You mean that's your girl, Mr. Bloom?"

"No. No, it isn't Avis. Now look—"

"Oh-oh," said Bernice, "I just stuck my foot in the old mouth-a-rooney there, didn't I?"

"Well look," said Avis, "if that's your girl, Mr. Bloom, maybe you oughta go in and talk to her because—"

"She is *not my girl*, Avis. *Not*," I said. "Now what seems to be the trouble?"

"I dunno," said Avis, "but she is probably the slowest undresser in the entire industry."

167

"I'd better go in and—"

"What the hell's going on here, a caucus?" said Landsdown, marching over to our little group. "Aren't you joining us in the altogether, Miss Baby?"

"Oh yeah, 'scuse me," said Bernice, unzipping her dress.

"And where's Alice?" said Landsdown. "Bloom, why aren't you supervising things here? *Alice!*"

"Yes?" said the voice of Alice.

"Come out here," said Landsdown, "we're ready to start."

"And here comes the llittle llady—nnnoww," said Bernice in a rough approximation of W. C. Fields.

"Alice, my dear," said Landsdown, "weren't you going to change clothes for this shooting?"

"Let's really hear it for her, folks," said Bernice, drawing off a stocking with an exaggerated gesture and flinging it insouciantly over her shoulder.

"I figured I'd keep my slip on until we're absolutely ready," said Alice, "due to the cold."

"What cold?" I said, "It's eighty-five degrees in here, for God's sake."

"Say," said Avis *sotto voce*, "you aren't Mr. Bloom's girl by any chance, areya, honey?"

"What?" said Alice.

"And here's a little souvenir of Atlantic City to take back home," said Bernice, continuing her act, draping her other stocking around my shoulders. "Tell 'em where ya got it, kid, and how easy it was."

168

"What's with *her?*" said Landsdown to me with a worried glance at Bernice, who was now bumping and grinding out of the rest of her lingerie.

"Youthful exuberance, sir," I said. "You know how these nutty college kids carry on."

Albert, seeing his mistress behaving in an abandoned fashion, figured it was playtime. He seized one end of the pink guaze bandage encircling Avis Hertz, gave it a vigorous tug which sent her spinning like a top as it unwound, and tore away on a mad circuit of the studio with the costume in his mouth.

"Hey," said Avis, spinning out and falling over on her side.

"Alice, we're absolutely ready *now,*" I said. "If you're too embarrassed, just say so."

"Oh, gee whiz," said Alice, tugging at her slip. "All right, but I'll probably catch pneumonia."

Just then, in walked Robbins.

"Well, I'll be damned," he said, looking happily around the room, from one undraped lady to the next, "I'll be God damned."

He hardly knew what to take in first. Then he saw me, his smile took a quizzical twist, and he joined the group.

"Hello, Bloom," he said, "what're you doing here?"

"Who's this?" said Landsdown.

"Oh," I said hurriedly, "Ralph Robbins, meet Fred Landsdown."

The two men shook hands carefully.

"They told me I'd find you here," said Robbins. "Thought I'd stop by and see the results of our ad. Things always about this lively?"

"Never," said Landsdown. "Seems to me it's the influence of Mr. Bloom here."

"Bloom?" said Robbins. "Why? What's he got to do with all this?"

An expectant hush had fallen over the entire assemblage.

"Well," said Landsdown, "it's Bloom who's—"

"—my lover, that's who he is," said Bernice, jumping into my arms.

"*What!*" said Alice.

"You mean *you're* Mr. Bloom's girl?" said Avis.

"*What* did you say you were?" said Alice, now nearly nude except for briefs and glasses. "*What* did you say you were?"

"Oliver's lady. His mistress. His concubine. His wench. Aren't I, Oll?"

I looked worriedly at Alice, then at Landsdown and Robbins, then decided it was a sacrifice play.

"Only in the sense that she shares my bed," I said.

Alice stopped hugging her bare midsection and gave me a hard openhanded crack on the side of the head. Then, red from head to toe, she grabbed somebody's dressing gown and raced out of the studio.

Pandemonium. Horses reared, ladies fainted, strong men cried.

"Well I'll be damned," said Robbins. "I'll be God damned."

170

"Are you *really* Mr. Bloom's girl?" said Avis.

"All right, all right!" said Landsdown. "That's enough. That's just about enough. The circus is over. Everybody go home."

"What about the shooting, sir?" I said.

"Home. Everbody go home. No shooting. Home."

"No shooting?" said Avis.

"No shooting?" said the photographer.

"The only shooting that'll be done around here today will be done by the police if I have to call them in to break up this riot," said Landsdown.

At the mention of the law, Robbins came to and began making his farewells.

"Really enjoyed it, Landsdown," he said, "Thanks a lot. Have to do it again some time."

"Not likely," said Landsdown.

"So long," said Robbins. "Seeya back at the office, Bloom."

"So long, sir," I called, and disengaged myself from Bernice.

"I've never seen anything like this before,'" said Landsdown.

"Rolf," said Albert.

"Get dressed, Al, we're going home," said Bernice.

"Who woulda guessed that was Mr. Bloom's girl," said Avis.

# 15

I didn't go back to the office right away. It was nearly lunchtime, so I walked into the nearest bar and had a Beefeater on rye. Then I dropped a couple of nickels in the public phone and dialed Alice's number.

"Hello?" said Alice.

"Alice, honey, I'd like to explain something," I said.

Click.

I dialed again.

"Don't hang up," I said. "I want to explain—"

Click.

I waited five minutes, then dialed again.

"Hello?" said Alice.

"Will you just give me ten seconds to explain something to you? Ten seconds?" I said.

"You have nothing to explain to me. I have nothing to explain to you. We have nothing to explain to each other. If you do not stop annoying me, I shall be forced to notify the proper authorities. Good day."

Click.

I waited five more minutes and dialed again.

"Hello?" said Alice.

*"The lady only said she was my mistress to save my job.* It was a desperation move to prevent Robbins and Landsdown from finding out about each other. *She* was the one who suffered public embarrassment, not you."

Silence at the other end. No click.

"I'd like to explain this more fully to you in person," I said.

"Who is this woman if not your mistress?"

"She is Mrs. Bernice Baby. She is the wife of Mr. Harry Baby of Santa Monica. She is my sister."

Pause.

"You swear this to be the truth?"

"Trust me," I said.

Pause.

"Thank you very much for calling, Mr. Bloom. If you do so once more, I promise you I shall notify the proper authorities. Good day."

"Alice? Wait, Alice—"

Click.

I shrugged and hung up.

A moment or so later, I picked up the phone and dialed again.

"*Hayday Magazine*, All The Nudes That's Fit To Print, good afternoon?"

"Oh, hi, Miss Selfridge, this is Oliver Bloom."

"Yes, Mr. Bloom."

"Is the old geezer in his office?"

"If Mr. Landsdown is the old geezer you are referring to, yes, he is."

"Good. Let me talk to him, would you?"

"I'm sorry, Mr. Bloom he's on another line. Will you hold?"

"Oh. Sure. No, wait. I'll call back in a little while."

"Very well, Mr. Bloom. Shall I tell him you called?"

"No, that's O.K. I'll try again in a little while."

I hung up, went back to the bar and had another Beefeater on rye. Then I went back to the phone and tried again.

"*Hayday Magazine*, All The Nudes That's Fit To Print, good afternoon?"

"Oh hi, it's me again. Is he off the line yet, Miss Selfridge?"

"Well, yes, he is, Mr. Bloom. But, if you'll permit me, I don't think it would be wise for you to speak to him just now."

"Why's that?"

"Well, he just got a telephone call which seemed to

upset him very greatly. I'm not certain, but I believe he's angry with *you,* Mr. Bloom."

"I see. Well, all right. Thanks for the tip, Miss Selfridge. Perhaps I'll just wait until this blows over, then."

"Yes sir. I think that might be best."

I went back to the bar and had another Beefeater.

"It's none of my business," said the bartender, "but you're throwing those drinks down like you was trying to drown your stomach."

"My good man," I said, "of *course* it's your business. Whose business is it if not yours? Here, let me buy you a whisky."

"You kidding me? I'd rather drink Lysol."

"What do you mean?" I said.

"You know what that stuff does to your insides? To your stomach? To your liver? To your kidneys? To your gall bladder? Feh!"

"What does it do?"

"It eats up all the tissues, that's what it does. It eats them up just like they was candy. You want to eat up your tissues, drink Lysol. It's faster."

"Wait a minute," I said. "You're a bartender, right? You make your living selling people drinks, right? How can you afford to speak this way about alcohol?"

"How can I afford? Listen, sonny, they pay me only to serve the drinks—to mix them and to serve them and that's all. To advertise them they don't pay me. For that they pay somebody else."

"If you hate alcohol so much, how come you're a bartender?"

"I can see you are very young. You think everybody does for a living what he likes? You think whatever a person likes to do somebody's going to pay him for? Is that what you think? Listen to me. A person does what he knows, not what he likes. It so happens I know how to mix drinks. Bingo, I'm a bartender. They didn't ask me if I like it when they hired me, only if I know how."

"I see," I said. "Well, that's certainly a very . . . remarkable outlook."

I ate up my my tissues a little more, then went back to the phone booth, dropped two nickels into the coin box and dialed. On a sudden whim, I hung up, reclaimed my nickels and went back to the bar.

"Listen," I said, slapping down two singles, "can you give me two bucks' worth of nickels?"

The bartender took the bills to the cash register and brought back the nickels.

"Who are you calling," he said, "the North Pole?"

"No, it's a local call. Say, could you possibly clean these nickels for me with a little soap and water?"

"You don't need to do that," said the bartender. "Lots of people make calls every day with dirty ones. The phone company don't care if you use dirty ones, believe me."

"Oh, I'm not going to put these nickels in the coin box," I said.

"You're not? Where are you going to put them?"

"In my mouth."

"In your mouth."

"Yes, in my mouth."

**177**

Pause.

"You're going to put the whole two dollars' worth of nickels right into your mouth?"

"That's right."

"Listen, sonny, it's none of my business, but don't do it. You want me to fix you another drink? Here, let me fix you another drink."

"I don't want another drink" I said, "I just want those nickels cleaned, if you don't mind."

"Here. Here's some nice Beefeater's. Drink it. It's on me. I'm paying for it out of my own pocket. Here."

"Please. Just clean the nickels. Otherwise I'll have to use them the way they are."

The bartender looked at me sadly for a moment, then sighed, shrugged, and rinsed off the nickels. "Here," he said. "You want me to dry them for you, too?"

"No, that's all right, thanks. They're just going to get wet again anyway."

He nodded.

I scooped up the nickels and filled my cheeks like some mercenary chipmunk.

"You want a little whisky to wash them down?" he said.

I shook my head and went back to the phone booth. I removed two nickels from my mouth, dropped them into the phone and dialed.

"*Hayday Magazine*, All The Nudes That's Fit To—"

"Mffr. Lanffdown, pleaff," I said.

"Excuse me?"

I removed about a dollar twenty from my cheeks.

"Mr. Landfdown, pleafe," I said.

"You wish to speak with Mr. Landsdown?"

"Yef."

"Whom shall I say is calling, please?"

"Treathury Department," I said, spitting out another forty-five cents, "the Bureau of Internal Revenue."

"Just a moment, please."

"Hello?" said Landsdown.

"Mr. Landsdown?"

"Yes?"

"Treasury Department here, Mr. Landsdown. Bureau of Internal Revenue. We're running a check on one of your employees. A Mr. O. Bloom?"

"Yes?"

"We are trying to ascertain his exact income. Would you happen to know if the salary you are currently paying him is his sole source of income?"

"I beg your pardon, but you sound like you've got a mouth full of nickels. Can I have that again?"

"I say would you know if he has any source of income other than the salary you pay him?"

"Another source of income, you say?"

"Yes. Do you know if he has one?"

"You're God damn right he has one. He has another full-time job at Plapper, Carstairs—at the advertising agency upstairs, that young son of a—Say, who am I speaking to over there, by the way?"

"Sir?"

"Who am I—Say, wait a minute. Bloom? Is this Bloom?"

"A Mr. O. Bloom is the party we are checking on, yes, sir."

Landsdown's voice took on a nasty edge.

"That's you, isn't it, Bloom?"

"No, sir, this is the Bureau of Internal—"

"Listen to me, Bloom. I want you to know what you've done is the lowest, crudest, sneakiest, filthiest, dirtiest, crookedest, most reprehensible thing I have ever heard of in my entire life. It's not enough that you deceived me by maintaining another full-time job. It's not enough that you were taking full pay from two employers and only putting in half a day's work for each in return. But you had the unmitigated, inexcusable, colossal lack of the commonest decency to maintain two full-time mistresses as well—and one of them scarcely more than a child. That I find absolutely unforgivable. That I find absolutely beyond my comprehension. Let me tell you something. If you ever dare to show your sneaky face around this office again, I will personally throw you bodily out of the building, and that's a promise. Do you hear me?"

"That's your final word on the matter?"

"That's my final fornicating word!"

"In that case," I said, "I resign."

Somehow I got back into my car and somehow I drove back home. Bernice found me parked outside, asleep at the wheel. She dragged me inside and put me to bed.

When I awoke, it was already dark. A fire was crackling merrily in the pseudo fireplace, the good dog Albert curled up contentedly on the pseudo hearth.

"Bernice?"

"Evening, pussycat. How do we feel?"

She sat down on the bed and scratched me behind the ears.

I purred.

Albert's ears went up, but he remained otherwise asleep.

"I'm sorry about this morning," she said.

"That's all right. It wasn't really your fault."

"Looks like it'll take a lot of talking to get old Alice back, eh?"

"The human larynx is not capable of the rate of talk it would take to get old Alice back. And I'm not really sure she'd be worth the trouble anyway."

"What do you mean?"

"Never mind. It's not important. I've just had a lousy day, honey, that's all."

"Oh, Oll, I'm so sorry."

She pulled back the covers, climbed underneath and snuggled up to me. I laid my head on her breast and kissed. She hugged. I hugged back. Before I knew it we were making love.

I hugged, I kissed, I fondled. I patted, I stroked, I squeezed. I pressed, rubbed, teased, licked, bit, chewed,

181

held, clenched, parted, thrust, entered, rode. I wanted to take her with me.

"Oliver," she whispered. "Oh, Oliver."

"Shhh."

She wanted so much to be a part of it. She wanted so much to make it happen. She tried very hard, and she stopped trying.

And then a curious thing. Bernice began to relax. I sensed it in a sigh. I felt it in her flesh. She had gone completely limp. And then. And then. Slowly, carefully, timidly at first, she seemed to have found the proper wave length, the proper signal. She seemed almost by accident to have tuned into the steady throbbing pulse that drives the universe, and, having found it, she hung onto it for dear life.

"Oliver Oliver Oliver," she whispered, "Oh my God, Oliver Bloom, please don't leave me behind again."

"Shhh."

Now she had it, now she'd finally found it. The pulse. The beat. The rhythm of life. Now she had it, now it had her. This was it. This was really it. Tears, yes. Sobs, yes. But I could feel the outlines of her smile against my face—the first real smile of her adult life was burned ineradicably into my cheek.

And then it was over. And even after, the pulse persisted, weaker, fading, ebbing, dying, now almost gone, now nearly gone, now gone, now entirely gone.

"Ollliverrr," she said. "Oh my."

"Bernice."

"Mmmmmmmmmmmmmmm."

Her eyes were closed. Her head rested lightly on the pillow. Her smile stretched from one ear to the other and back again.

"Oh my," she said, "My my my my my."

She giggled. She chortled. She belly-laughed.

"My my," she said, "Bernice Baby has finally become a big lady. Bernice Baby has finally grown up."

We got up out of bed and toasted her womanhood with hot honey and lemon juice.

I awoke the next morning to hollowness. There was a hollow in the bed beside me. There was a hollow in my chest. The very house was hollow. And then I remembered: "Bernice Baby has finally grown up." I didn't even need to look for her. I knew that she was gone.

Bernice in full bloom had burst out of her boll, which, though it had brought her to maturity, was now no longer large enough to contain her.

I tunneled under the covers, hoping to trap a few last calories of warmth, but instead found only cold sheets and emptiness.

Ah, Bernice: I cannot really blame you, but I can surely pity the hell out of me.

I lay in the bed I had made, three sheets to the wind and foundering in a sea of mixed metaphors. Then I stretched, got up and chewed my way through half a package of dry Wheat Chex and six Ritz crackers.

I considered calling Robbins. Would he have heard from Landsdown by now? Probably. I wasn't really ready to face him yet.

183

I climbed, unshaven, into my clothes and into my car. I went for a drive in the hills.

The sun had not dawned that day. It was crouching just over the horizon with morning sickness. The sky, a yellowish-grayish mess which would have preferred to remain black, sniffled once or twice and began to drip.

I rolled up the windows, turned on the wipers and listened to the spatter on the canvas roof as the end-of-the-affair hemingway heavens opened up and the rain came down in ernest.

I wound out of the hills down to Sunset, turning west toward the ocean, following the world-famous and little-known boulevard through garishness, through hedge-hidden suburban manors, through wild, wooded, twisting turns to emerge ultimately in more garishness where Sunset hit the Coast Highway. I headed south then, as rain slanted into the lead-colored Pacific, water returning to water.

Lots of roadside seaside fish shacks, lots of orangey fish-shaped neon signs. Fresh clam, crab, scallop, shrimp, shark, squid, swordfish, sand dab, mussel, grunion, oyster, lobster (flown in daily from Maine).

And then the beach towns. Peeling clapboard summer cottages lived in all year round by people who like the feel of sand between their toes (and sheets), people who wear sandals to work, who drink Pepsi and think young, the sun-bleached, waterlogged, middle-aged teen-agers of Southern California.

And between the summer houses, roadside shacks and neon fish: the oil wells—huge iron replicas of those

184

toy-store bobbing birds, ceaselessly dipping that greasy kid stuff out of the earth.

The rain grew heavy. My gas gauge read near empty —not surprising since I had already come a great distance and was averaging an honest five miles to the gallon in order to feed the three or four hundred odd horses with steaming flanks who labored so nobly under my hood.

I cut the engine and hissed into a filling station.

No courteous uniformed attendant with leather bow tie and billboard smile came bounding out to greet me.

Inside a well-lit glass cage, two lads in jump suits drank steaming coffee and dawdled over Chinese checkers.

I tooted my horn.

One of the men looked up, said something to the other, who looked up also, then both returned to the more immediate and drier work of bounding over marbles.

I honked again.

Both men looked up again. One waved.

I leaned on the horn.

Finally, one of them shrugged, stood up and opened the door.

"What you want?" he yelled.

"Gas!" I yelled.

He turned to the other man and shared with him the humor of my request.

"It's raining!" he yelled.

"So what?"

"So we ain't got no raincoats. Come back when it stops."

"I can't come back. I don't have any more gas."

He turned to the other man for a quick conference, then back to me.

"C'mon inside," he said, motioning me into the glass cage.

I snorted, sighed, turned up my collar and made a break for the doorway.

"Sit down," said the one who'd invited me in.

I shook off the wet like a puppy and sat down on the chrome and plastic chair offered me.

"Want some coffee?" said the other man.

"No thanks. Look, can't I just get some gas and be on my way?"

"You in a big hurry to get somewheres, are ya?"

"Well . . . not exactly, but—"

"Then relax. It'll let up soon."

"You mean you don't ever service cars when it rains?"

The one I had addressed turned to the other.

"Hey, Floyd, when's the last time it rained here—you recall?"

Floyd gave it some serious thought.

"I don't recollect as how it's *ever* rained since I've been here," he said.

"How long have you been here?"

Floyd gave it some more serious thought.

"I'd say mebbe three, four years, on the inside."

"Three or four years? You're telling me it hasn't rained here in three or four years?"

**186**

"On the inside."

"And what's your outside guess?"

"Outside?"

"Yes."

He turned to the other man.

"What's our outside guess?"

"Oh, let me see. I'd say about . . . two weeks, on the outside."

"Two *weeks* on the outside?" I said.

"Yep. It rains a whole lot more on the outside than on the inside around these parts," he said, and both of them dropped to the tiles in whoops of laughter.

"I see," I said. "Well, that's certainly very amusing. Look, how soon will it be before you can fill up my tank?"

"On the outside?" said Floyd, and broke himself up all over again.

I arose.

"Where ya goin'?" said the one who wasn't Floyd.

"To find a service station," I said.

"Aw. Wait a minute. We was only having a little fun. We just wanted to see whether you was a good sport or not, wasn't we, Floyd?"

"That's very true," said Floyd. "That's all we wanted to see."

"Well, it so happens I'm a *lousy* sport. O.K.? Now, are you going to sell me some gas or aren't you?"

"Sure we will."

"When?"

"Soon as the rain lets up. We told you."

187

I went to the door.

"The next service station," said Floyd, "is a good fifteen, sixteen miles down the road."

"On the inside," said the one who wasn't Floyd.

"Judging by what you're driving," said Floyd, "I doubt if you'd make it that far even on a full tank."

"I don't believe it's fifteen miles to the next service station," I said.

"Yeah, you're right. It's probably more like twenty."

"Well, I'll just chance it," I said, opening the door.

"Some service station attendants," said Floyd, "have been known to feel so bitter toward a customer as to call all the stations down the road and ask them not to wait on him."

"I don't believe it. They have to wait on everybody. It's the law."

"Not," said Floyd, "on unruly customers who have caused a scene and spoke in an abusive manner to the kindly attendant who waits on them."

"That's very true," said the one who wasn't Floyd. "Section 225-2G of the California Retail Merchants Code."

I narrowed my eyes at him.

"You'd make up a story like that?" I said.

"Us? Heck no. Not us. We'd never do a thing like that," he said, turning to the other man, "would we?"

"Heck no."

"Heck no," said Floyd. "Some would, though, I guess."

"Some sure would," said the other.

188

"All right," I said, pulling out my wallet. "How much do you two gentlemen want to go out there and fill up my car?"

The two men looked at each other in astonishment.

"Mister," said the one who wasn't Floyd, "do you seriously think I and Floyd has been holding out all this time for a bribe? Is that what you think?"

"Mister," said Floyd, "we are very deeply offended."

"That's very true," said the other man. "I can't remember when I have ever been more personally hurt."

"All right," I said, "then what *are* you holding out for?"

"For the rain to stop, for one thing," said Floyd.

"And for a little pleasant conversation with an interesting and worth-while human being, for another," said the other.

"It gets mighty boring here, just the two of us," said Floyd. "We'd be much obliged if you'd sit a spell, accept a cup of our coffee and chat with us."

"We'd be very much obliged," said the other. "And when the rain lets up, we'll even fill up your tank."

I sighed and sat back down.

"That's better," said Floyd. "Now then, cream or sugar?"

"Black," I said.

"Good. We don't have cream or sugar. Now go right ahead and tell us all about yourself."

"I just don't understand how you can be so picky about when and how you sell your gas and still stay in business," I said.

189

"Oh, that's the smallest part of our business, pumping gas, isn't it, Floyd?"

"That's very true," said Floyd. "We specialize more in lube jobs and wheel balancing and selling tires and car wax and running rest rooms. Pumping gas don't hardly amount to five percent of our business."

"We was even thinking about taking out the gas pumps entirely."

"Heck," said Floyd, "that's enough about us. Now tell us about you. What line of work you in?"

"I work for an advertising agency and I used to work for a magazine."

"What magazine?"

"*Hayday.*"

"*Hayday?* The one with all the broads? You worked for them, honest?"

"That's right."

"How do you like that! Tell us about it. Tell us about all the orggies."

"Orgies. There weren't any."

"What do you mean, there weren't any?"

"There weren't any."

"Aw. C'mon. Tell us. We won't repeat any of it. Nobody but him and me will ever know."

"I wish I could tell you that there were, but the fact is that there weren't. A few largely uninteresting shooting sessions, some less predictable than others perhaps, and the rest just plain office work. No orgies. No gangbangs. Not even a simple roll in the hay."

"Aw."

"It's true. Everyone seems to feel that working on a girlie magazine is one huge orgy. Well, it's not. It's a very serious business, and it's a hell of a lot of work. Do you see naked women there? Of course you do. But you see so many that the novelty wears off in the first week. By the second week, you're paying more attention to the ones with clothes. Ever been to a nudist colony? Most boring place in the world. No mystery. Nothing left to the imagination. A nudist colony is the most puritanical society you'll ever see."

Silence.

"I don't believe you," said Floyd. "I don't believe you even worked for them."

"Have you got a copy of *Hayday* around anywhere?" I said.

"There's one over by the Coke machine."

I went over to the Coke machine, picked up the magazine, opened it to the masthead and laid it on the table in front of them. Then I took out my driver's license and laid it alongside.

"Please note the similarity of the name on the license to that of the name where it says 'Art Director,'" I said.

They both noted.

"Satisfied?" I said.

"There could be two Oliver Blooms."

I went to the Coke machine, brought back the five phone books of the Greater Los Angeles Area, opened each in turn to the Blooms and laid them alongside the license and the magazine.

191

"Please note. Only one Oliver Bloom in the Greater Los Angeles Area. His address in the phone book is the same one as appears on my driver's license. Now are you satisfied?"

"You may be the Oliver Bloom on the driver's license and you may also be the Oliver Bloom in the phone book, but that don't mean you're the *real* Oliver Bloom. The one in the magazine."

"Look," I said. "The magazine is published in Hollywood, right? How could the real Oliver Bloom not live in the Greater Los Angeles Area? You think he commutes every day from Seattle?"

"Maybe he has an unlisted number," said Floyd.

"Aah, he's telling the truth about who he is, Floyd. He's just fooling about the orggies."

"Orgies. Look," I said, "I'll tell you what. I'll tell you the truth about the orgies if you'll promise to take care of my car before it stops raining? Deal?"

"Deal!" said Floyd, coming to life again.

"Deal!" said his friend happily.

"Well, first of all," I said, leaning back in my chair, "everybody in the office has to take off all their clothes the minute they come to work. You know how most offices have coat racks? We have a locker room. If it is unusually breezy out, the girls are permitted to wear their panties."

"Oh boy," said Floyd.

"How *about* that," said his friend.

"Of course," I said, "visitors would feel out of place if they were the only ones wearing clothes, so the minute they come in, the receptionist stands up and helps them get undressed."

"Hot damn," said Floyd.

"Tell us about the banging," said his friend.

"Well," I said, "there's a company rule that every woman who works for us, as a model or even as a secretary, has to go to bed with every man on the staff during her first week on the job, to sort of get acquainted. Then, every girl must spend at least one night per month with either me or the editor/publisher, Fred Landsdown, apart from the biweekly interoffice orgy."

"Golly Mo," said Floyd. "What's that?"

"Well, the biweekly interoffice orgy, or B.W.I.O.O., as we call it, is held in our main orgy-room on the second and fourth Fridays of every month. It starts promptly at five P.M."

"When does it end?"

"Monday at nine."

"Holey Moley," said Floyd.

"I'll be jiggered," said his friend.

"Now, I'll tell you what happens at a typical B.W.I.O.O. the minute you've finished filling my car. Deal?"

"Deal," said Floyd.

"Deal," said his friend. "We knew you was just fooling when you said there wasn't no orggies before."

"We can generally tell when a man is fooling on us," said Floyd.

"I can see you're pretty good judges of character," I said, following them out the door into the rain.

193

# 16

The moment I walked in the door the telephone rang.

"Hello?"

"Mr. Bloom?"

"Yes?"

"This is the office calling."

"Which office?"

"PKC&R."

"Oh. Yes?"

"We were wondering what happened to you. You didn't come back to the office yesterday and you didn't show up at all today. We've been calling you all afternoon. Are you all right?"

"Oh. Yes. I mean, no, I'm not."

"What's wrong, are you sick?"

"Well, sort of. Nothing serious, really. I just got back from the U.C.L.A. Medical Center, as a matter of fact."

"What did they say?"

"They said . . . to get back into bed and drink plenty of liquids."

"Oh, then you have the flu?"

"Something like that."

"Mr. Robbins is very disturbed about you."

"You mean because I haven't called in sick or for some other reason?"

"I don't know, I just know he's very disturbed."

"Oh. Well, I'm dreadfully sorry I wasn't able to call, but I wasn't even conscious for a good part of the time, you see."

"My goodness! How did you get to the Medical Center?"

"I . . . managed. I drove very slowly. Every time I felt I was losing consciousness, I just pulled over to the side of the road. That makes for slow going, but it's not so bad if you're careful."

"My goodness! Do you want us to send someone over to take care of you?"

"That won't be necessary," I said. "Just tell Mr. Robbins I'll be in as soon as the fever drops off."

"Very well, Mr. Bloom. And be sure to let us know if there's anything we can do for you."

"I will," I said. "Thanks for calling."

I hung up the telephone, sat down on the bed, spread out my thoughts on the fuzzy imitation orlon blanket and commenced to take stock: In a really surprisingly short time I had gone through positively one and possibly two perfectly good jobs, as well as two ladies in perfectly good condition—one late model, hardly used, and one older job, nicely rebuilt at great personal expense.

I attempted an assessment of my feelings. *Hayday:* Hayday I would surely miss, for at least another fifteen minutes. PKC&R: PKC&R I might miss for another week. Alice: Alice I stopped missing the instant I learned of her grudge call to Friendly Fred. Bernice: Ah, Bernice. Bernice was the most unkind cut of all, the one loss I truly found it hard to rationalize. Perhaps it was significant that she was the only one not lost through the wages of sneakiness. (Oh what a tangled web we weave when first we learn to juggle a pair of professions and a brace of broads.)

But how had I lost Bernice? What had been my crime? ("Your honor, we find the defendant guilty on three counts of overindulgence, five counts of unreasonable patience and seventeen separate counts of extreme and excessive mental and physical tenderness.") Yargh. I lay down and drew my self-pity up about my ears.

Well, matters might not be so miserable after all. Maybe Bernice would see the error of her ways and come back to me. Sure, and maybe Mao Tse-tung would see the error of his ways and apply for U.S. citizenship.

Ah, the hell with her. Whether she realized it or not, she'd had a pretty sweet thing going for her with me. Yeah. I *was*, after all, a fairly pleasant-looking fellow, in my own wiry way. I *was*, after all, a fairly skillful chap in the old sack. I *was*, after all, a fairly good provider. How many men could give her what I could—an open-beamed roof over her head, a natural shoulder on which to lay her head, a season's pass to the Hughes Market, and full kennel facilities? How many men could offer her that? Not so many, that's how many. So, if she didn't know a good thing when she saw one, who needed her anyway? Who needed a lady with lousy taste?

One thing was certain. I certainly wasn't going to lie around the house and wait for her to come back. No, sir, I certainly wasn't going to do that. What I *was* going to do, I was going to roll right over, pick up the telephone, dial a few numbers and get to know a few new ladies, that's what.

I rolled over, picked up the phone, dialed a few numbers and waited for the first new lady to answer.

"Hello, lady," I said to the first new lady. "My name is Oliver Bloom and what I would most like you to tell me, aside from the general condition of your health, is whether or not you have a listing for a Miss or Mrs. Bernice Baby."

"Surely. May I have that name again, please?"

"Baby. B-A-B-Y. Baby, Bernice."

"Surely. Baby is the first name or the last, please?"

"The last, the last."

"Surely. I have an Exbrook exchange in Santa Monica. Would that be it, sir?"

"No, that's the old one. Don't you have a more recent listing? Could you check a few other areas?"

"Surely. One moment, please."

I tried unspiraling the telephone cord. Very difficult. I tried spiraling it. Easier.

"How are you coming there, miss? You still with me?"

"Surely. I am sorry, sir, but I have no other listing for that party."

"Did you check all five areas? Are you sure?"

"Surely. There is no other listing for that party, sir."

"I see."

Maybe it was still too soon. Maybe Bernice hadn't installed a phone in the new place yet.

"Miss, how long, on the average, does it take to install a telephone?"

The lady's voice changed gears.

"You wish to install a telephone, sir?"

"No no, I just wanted to know how long it took."

"We could be out within the hour, sir. Just give me your name and address and—"

"I said no, I only wanted to—"

"Of course you'll want to have our dainty Princess model, sir, which—"

"No. I don't want your dainty Princess model."

"Very well, what color would you prefer in the regular model, sir? We have beige, plum, fuchsia—"

"I don't want *any* color in the regular model."

"Very well, black it is. Now then, we have twenty-five-foot cord, the thirty-five-foot length, the hundred-foot length, and the special step-saving half-mi—"

I hung up. The telephone wasn't the only way to find a person. There would be other ways. Eventually they would come to me.

The following afternoon I got back into my car and tooled down Laurel Canyon Boulevard. In my head an idea was beginning to pat itself into shape. *Sure* there was no listing for Bernice in the phone book—she hadn't planned to leave so soon. It had been a spontaneous move, and it would take her at least a week to find an apartment and put in a phone. In the meantime she had to be in a motel.

By continually doubling back on yourself between Wilshire and Olympic boulevards, proceeding westerly from Laurel Canyon, it is possible to hit eighty-seven motels before you reach the Pacific Ocean. I don't know the record time for such a run, but it took me three and a half hours.

In the eighty-seven motel registers I'd scanned, I turned up six Bernices, fifty-two babies, and not a single Bernice Baby. Either Mr. Keen knew something I didn't, or else it used to take him a lot longer than his thirty-minute radio programs to trace lost persons. I pulled into the dark parking lot at State Beach and slumped as far down as you can slump in a bucket seat.

Somewhere in the hundreds of square miles behind

me, a lady and a dog shared supper hamburgers on the threshold of a brave new world—a world where all things were possible, including True Love on a white charger. What if I *did* find them? Would I be able to convince them their quest was futile? Would I be able to persuade them to come back—that the only white charger they'd ever need in this vale of tears was the Diner's Club card of Oliver Bloom?

Whatever my chances, I obviously couldn't talk Bernice and Albert into returning unless I found them first. If I waited a week or two till they located an apartment and installed a phone, perhaps I could find them by calling Information. But what if they located an apartment and didn't install a phone? Or what if they couldn't locate an apartment at all and decided to leave town?

I couldn't wait any week or two, I had to find them now. But where to look? Whom to ask? Come to think of it, there was one person who just might know. No, not just *might* know—*must* know. If Harry was in the process of divorcing her, either he or his lawyer had to know where to get in touch with her.

Yes. No doubt about it. The old Bernice might not have been so conscientious as to stay in touch, but the new Bernice—the one who had outgrown me—she would proceed with the divorce and would keep the lawyer informed of her whereabouts.

It was simply a matter of going to Harry and (employing a certain measure of delicacy, to be sure) finding out where she was. How simple. How perfectly simple it all was when you could think things out logically. In a matter of hours I would see Bernice once more. I would plead my case eloquently, brilliantly, tenderly, and she could not fail to see that the only sensible course would be to come back with me to my—to our little castle in the canyon.

Were Round-Table romantics the only way to win the heart of Lady Bernice? Then perhaps I would sally forth and slay me a dragon (or reasonable facsimile thereof) before I went to plight my troth.

I turned the key in the ignition, put my ponies in gear, and tore out of the parking lot with a flourish of klaxons.

The building when I got there seemed deserted, though the doors were still unlocked. I entered the elevator and rode to seven, then alighted and made my way down the empty corridor.

Please be here, Robbins, I prayed—it will be a hollow victory if you are not present to defend yourself.

I strode up to his door and flung it open. He was, unfortunately, in.

"Bloom! What the hell are *you* doing here?"

"Oh. Uh, well . . ."

"They told me you were sick."

Already I could see that it was not going to go well. It was not too late to withdraw, to mumble something about emotional illness, refer him to my analyst and plead for mercy on the grounds of insanity. ("You see, sir, the Oliver Bloom you hired was never even *aware* of

202

the Oliver Bloom at *Hayday*. He was— I am—they are —a schizophrenic personality.") No, that was the coward's way. I must be brave. For Lady Bernice.

"Sick, Robbins? You're damned right I'm sick. Sick of hypocrisy, sick of deceit. Sick of living a lie for I do not know how many months. So now you know, and I can at last lay down my burden of guilt. But wait. Maybe I'm not so guilty after all. Maybe the only injury you incurred was to your corporate ego."

"What do you mean?"

"Have you ever, up until now, known me to miss a copy deadline?"

"Well, no, but—"

"Have you ever felt that my creative output was in any way smaller than that of your full-time writers?"

"Look, Bloom, I—"

"Answer the question!"

"Well, no, but—"

"Aha! You see? So why am I being fired?"

"Fired?"

"Yes, fired."

"Fired is not really the word, Bloom. You see—"

"Oh no you don't. Don't you give me that We-hate-to-let-you-go-but-we've-got-to-tighten-our-belts routine. Let's call a spade a spade, fella. Let's just have a little straight talk here. Are you or are you not replacing me with another writer?"

"Well, yes, but—"

"Aha! And this despite the fact that the quantity and quality of my work have been beyond reproach."

"Who said anything about quality?"

"Huh?"

"I said your *quantity* was beyond reproach, I didn't say a thing about quality. Frankly, Bloom, your copy has never exactly danced its way into my heart."

"Oh . . . I see. I thought . . . I thought I was being fired because you found out I was also on Fred Landsdown's payroll."

"What? You were?"

"You mean you didn't know?"

"What were you doing for him?"

"For Landsdown? I was his art director. I thought you knew that."

"How the hell did you manage to hold two jobs at once?"

"I just traded off between you—a couple hours here, a couple hours there. I thought you knew that."

"Wait a minute. That explains what you were doing at that shooting!"

"Well, sure, but—"

"I'll be God damned. I'll just be God damned. Two full-time jobs. That's the sneakiest thing I've ever heard of, Bloom."

"Yes sir. Well, I realize that, but—"

"You know, I was going to offer you a job as an art director. An opening came up and, knowing your background, I figured you've *got* to be a better art director than a writer. But after hearing this—"

"Oh, but you see, sir, that's all over now. I'm through with deceit and—"

"—I know exactly what I want to do with you."

"Uh . . . what?"

"Bloom, how'd you like to be a mirror man?"

"A what?"

"A mirror man. You may not have heard yet, but ours, who was known to the Throb people as Steve, has just accepted a job as Scantlebury's ad manager. I was really stuck for somebody sneaky enough to replace him until now, but I really think you could handle it. How's about it, kid—think you'd like the job? It pays more than twice your old salary."

Pause. Think. Shift. Speak.

"Uh, actually, Robbins, what I came to see you about was our man Steve. I mean, personally, Steve is one of my favorite people, sir. That is, I think he's a very sweet guy and all, but he does seem to have an awful lot of problems. I also think that, under the present circumstances, anyone here—even I—could do a better job as mirror man."

"Beautiful!" said Robbins, pounding my back, "Beautiful!"

I smiled becomingly.

"That was just off the top of my head, sir."

"You kidding me? You're *beautiful*, Bloom. Listen, a few pointers from me and you're going to know the secret of how to cloud men's minds better than Lamont Cranston himself. Tell you what. I'll teach you everything I know if you'll just do me one tiny favor in return."

"What's that?"

205

"Describe to me in glorious detail every orgy you guys ever threw at *Hayday*. I'm out of my skull with curiosity. Deal?"

"But we never *had* any orgies at *Hay*— Deal, sir," I said.

Covered with glory, I entered the elevator. I started to push the button marked one, and then I did a curious thing. I pushed the button marked five instead.

The elevator dropped, the doors opened, and I was in the offices of *Hayday Magazine*. Well, I thought—if one dragon, why not two?

I stalked up to Landsdown's office, kicked open the door, and was not at all surprised to see him at his desk.

"Landsdown," I said, "I have just come to tell you that, although it is true I held another job while in your employ, I did you no disservice and, hence, feel no longer any burden of guilt. It has further struck me that the only sort of injury you might have incurred as a result of this experience was to your corporate ego. So let's call a spade a spade, fella. Let's face facts. I was a hell of a great art director, and although I no longer need you, you still damn well need me. Therefore, here is what I propose: I shall continue to direct *Hayday's* artwork on retainer, I shall put in half my former number of hours, and you will pay me double my former salary. What do you say—is it a deal?"

Landsdown remained absolutely motionless for perhaps twenty seconds. Then he stood up, came around his desk with hand extended, bums-rushed me all the way to the elevator and dropped me on the floor in front of it.

"I told you once and I'll tell you again," said Landsdown. "If you ever dare to show your face around this office, I will personally throw you bodily out of the building. Do you hear me?"

"I hear you, I hear you," I said from the floor. "Big goddam deal."

At street level I slapped myself free of dust, lowered myself into the saddle once more and, sword slightly bent, adjusted my visor and headed for Harry's house.

It was going on ten o'clock as I dismounted and rang the doorbell.

"Oll! Well, how*about* that! Come on in, boy!"

I might as well have been his long lost Siamese twin. He had no right to be so glad to see me.

"Hiya, Harry."

I followed him inside.

"Gee, Oll, howya been?"

"Oh, pretty fair. How about yourself?"

"Can't complain, can't complain. Sit down, Oll, old man. Take a load off."

I sat down and took a load off.

"There," he said, "that's better. Now what can I fix you?"

"Fix me? Oh, I don't really want anything to drink, thanks."

His smile sagged.

"However, I will have a little scotch on the rocks if

you insist," I added hastily, noting with satisfaction the return of his smile.

"Well, let's see what we got," he said and went to the liquor cabinet.

"So what have you been up to, Harry?"

"Oh, you know. This and that, this and that. How's about some bourbon, Oll? Bourbon sound good to ya, ha?"

"Oh, sure. Bourbon's fine."

"O.K., Oll. Bourbon coming right up, boy."

Harry poured some bourbon into a couple of glasses.

"Hey, Oll, what do you like with it? Ya want soda with it or ginger ale or what?"

"Oh. Yeah, sure. Ginger ale is fine."

"Right, Oll. Ginger ale coming right up."

Harry went into the kitchen and made icebox noises.

"Hey, Oll?"

"Yeah?"

"There doesn't seem to be anything here to mix it with. Not unless you want it with clam juice, that is."

"Oh. Well that's O.K. Don't worry about it."

"What?"

"I said fine. I'll just drink it straight."

"Oh. I mean, you don't want the clam juice, then, is that it?"

"No, that's O.K. I'd prefer it straight, actually."

"Right. I guess I'll have mine straight, too."

Harry came back into the living room, handed me a glass and sat down.

"So what've you been up to, Oll?"

"Oh, this and that," I said, "this and that."

This and that wasn't going to get the job done. I decided to be direct.

"Harry, can I speak frankly? Can I speak man to man?"

"Why, sure, Oll. What's on your mind?"

"Well, I don't know whether you know this, but Bernice has been living with me for several months now. She moved in with me a few days after you kicked her out."

"After I what?"

"After you kicked her out."

"Is that what she told you?"

"Why . . . yes. Didn't you kick her out?"

"If that's what she said. Go on. What else?"

"Oh. Well, anyway, we'd been living together for several months and we—well, I, at any rate, had begun to feel a rather deep personal attachment for her. Then, quite suddenly, either early yesterday morning or late in the evening the night before last, she left. Disappeared, kit and kaboodle. Or, *dog* and kaboodle, if you prefer. I've tried to locate her by looking in motels but it's kind of a hopeless task, as you can well imagine. At any rate, I hoped that you might have some idea of where she's hiding out."

"What do you want her for?" said Harry quite seriously.

"What do I want her for? I don't know. I guess I probably love her. I guess I probably want to marry her or something."

"You can't do that," said Harry.

"I can't? Why not?"

"She's already married."

"Oh. Well, after the divorce, I mean."

"After what?"

"After the divorce. You . . . *are* divorcing her, aren't you?"

"Is that what she told you?"

"Why yes. Isn't it true? Didn't you start divorce proceedings against her?"

"If that's what she said. Go on. What else?"

"That's all. Nothing else. I just thought you might know where she went, that's all. Apparently you don't."

I was beginning to sense that I was no longer his long lost Siamese twin. I bolted the bourbon and stood up.

"I do know where she is," said Harry.

"You do?"

"Yes."

"Where?"

Harry pointed to the rug. I looked at it stupidly.

"What do you mean?" I said.

"Here. Bernice is here. With me."

I sat down.

"What do you mean?" I said.

"I mean she came back here early yesterday morning. She said she wanted me to take her back. She said she had learned her lesson. She said she wanted to call off the divorce."

"And?"

"And I agreed."

"I see," I said.

I stood up rather carefully, then sat down again rather hard.

"I see," I said.

"I'm sorry, Oll."

"Yes. Well, no harm done. I'm . . . I'm afraid I have to, uh, leave now."

I stood up, made it to the door, opened it and walked outside without looking back.

"I'm sorry, Oll," said Harry from the doorway. "I really am."

I walked down the street to the car, walked on past it, crossed over to the next block and just kept on walking. It was a beautiful night and you could smell orange blossoms and lemons and grapefruit in people's yards, and there didn't seem to be the slightest reason to ever stop walking.

I was aware of salt and eventually I was aware of spray and of the sound of the breakers as they thudded into the flat hard sand. I was aware of the hiss of the shattered waves as they were sucked back for successive attacks on the shore line. Hiss . . . pause . . . thunder. Hiss . . . pause . . . thunder.

I sat down in the cold sand and leaned my back against a wooden lifeguard stand. Every seventh wave has extra power, say the surfers. If you listen closely you can even hear the difference after a while. Hiss, pause, thunder. Hiss, pause, thunder. Extra power for what? ("Housewives: Now there's a new wave with extra cleaning power, and you can actually *hear the difference*. Ask for Seventh Wave at your nearest Atlantic or Pacific Ocean.") Hiss, pause, thunder. Hiss, pause, thunder. All night long I advertised and counted waves.

# 17

I hadn't been aware of falling asleep and I also hadn't been aware of waking, but whether I had slept or not the sky was now bright and the sea gulls were wheeling and dealing and doing whatever it is that sea gulls do early on a sunny morning by the sea.

I sat as I had the night before, with my back against the lifeguard stand, now watching the waves that I could only hear the night before. If I had been at home

I might have gotten up and gotten dressed and washed my face. But I was not at home, and since I was already up and dressed and since the spray had washed my face all night, I saw no need to do anything but sit with my back against the lifeguard stand and watch the waves.

By and by, a nice slender lady who was not quite pretty came walking down the sand by the water with a nice German shepherd who was not quite a pure German shepherd but who carried himself nicely.

The not quite pure German shepherd spotted my narrow white salt-caked body and frolicked over. Straddling my torso, he vigorously licked my face and wagged my knees with his tail.

The not quite pretty lady approached uncertainly.

"Oll? Oliver, is that you?"

She knelt down and examined me through my coating of salt.

When I tried to speak, my equipment sounded as though it hadn't been used in years.

"Hello, lady," I cackled.

"Pussycat, you look awful. What are you doing here?"

"I live here, lady. I'm a lifeguard."

She took a handkerchief out of her coat pocket, moistened it with her tongue and dabbed at the spots on my face that Albert had missed.

"Oll honey, you don't look at all well. I'm taking you home. Can you stand up by yourself?"

She took my hand and tugged gently.

"Leave me be, lady. I'm needed here at my post."

"For what?"

214

"For saving lives."

"Yeah? The shape you're in, you couldn't save Green Stamps. Come on, let's go home. I'll make you chicken soup."

"Whose home? Yours? Mine? Whose?"

"Yours and mine. Ours. O.K.?"

"I don't understand," I said, not having understood. "I thought you went back to Harry. I thought you left me to go back to Harry."

"Who told you that?"

"Harry."

"Harry's full of lemon drops. I haven't seen him in months."

"I don't get it. Why would Harry lie to me? Harry never used to lie to anybody."

"How should *I* know why he lied to you? I told you he's changed. Maybe he thought he was doing you a favor—protecting you from yourself, or from the nut Bernice. Maybe he's just taking a little revenge. He's entitled."

Hmmm.

"If you didn't leave me to go back to Harry then why did you leave me?"

"To think."

"About what?"

"True Love."

"What did you decide?"

"That I couldn't decide."

"I see." Pause. "Bernice?"

"Yes?"

"I love you. I'm up to my ears in love with you."

Pause.

"I know."

"Oh. Bernice?"

"Yes?"

"Do you love me?"

Pause. Long pause.

"I guess so."

"Then say it. Say, 'I love you, Oliver Bloom.'"

Pause. Softly:

"I love you, Oliver Bloom."

"Bernice?"

"Yes?"

"Would you . . . would you like to be my wife?"

Pause.

"After the divorce, you mean?"

"Yes."

"For better or for worse? In sickness and in health? Till death do us part, you mean?"

"Yes."

"Can Albert come too?"

"Yes."

"In that case, it's a deal," she said, and she and Albert came tumbling into my arms.

We hugged and kissed and said nice things and the three of us cried like babies.